ACCLAIM FOR OUT OF

"While I was growing up in Brooklyn, Jerome Kass was growing up in the Bronx. We should have met. We had a lot to discuss. *Out of the Bronx* is as much about my Italian-American world as it is about his Jewish-American world. Sensitively written, painfully funny, and painfully sad, his book captures growing up in the Forties and Fifties as well as anything I've ever read."
— Nick Pileggi, Author of *Wiseguy*, *Casino*, and *Goodfellas*

"Jerry Kass always writes from the heart. He hitches real life to his pages—real people who love, yearn, fight, drive each other insane, make family. *Out of the Bronx* is the latest example of his compassionate talent for observation and story telling."
— Susan Stamberg, Special Correspondent, National Public Radio

"Jerome Kass embodies the wit and wisdom of J.D. Salinger and Henry Roth to tell the story of Joel Sachs and his family, a Bronx tale from a by-gone era. I felt that I knew these people—their rages, their dreams, their claustrophobic apartment—because a long time ago, I did know these people. Kass has not imagined them; he has exhumed them. There is poignant truth here, a story masterfully told by a master storyteller. I finished *Out of the Bronx* with sadness. I felt at home in it."
— Richard Cohen, Columnist, *The Washington Post*

"Jerome Kass's *Out of the Bronx* brilliantly takes you through Joel Sachs and his family's life together over the years, chapter by chapter, story by story. With great insight and honesty, Kass lets you see how funny, sexy, sad, and wonderful it all is—just like life itself. I thoroughly enjoyed the journey and I'm still thinking about this family, especially Fanny."
— Julie Kavner, Actress on *Rhoda*, in six Woody Allen films, and the voice of Marge on *The Simpsons*

"Not since Philip Roth's early work have I read such an exciting book about the difficulties of growing up in New York. *Out of the Bronx* is filled with compassion, pathos, and humor. Jerome Kass has given us a cast of unforgettable characters and placed them in his old neighborhood with masterful detail. This is a read you won't soon forget."
— John Erman, Award-winning director of *Roots* and
   An Early Frost

"J.D. Salinger, move over. Philip Roth, make room. The dysfunctional Sachs family of the Bronx is as entertaining as the Glass family of Manhattan and the comically compulsive hero, Joel Sachs, matches Alex Portnoy of Newark stroke for stroke. Jerome Kass's bildungsroman is artful, moving, and very funny. I enjoyed it immensely; I commend it heartily."
— Josh Greenfeld, Author of *A Child Called Noah*

"This sad, funny, thoroughly absorbing collection of stories by Jerry Kass reads like a novel. You may not wish you were a member of this highly dysfunctional family, but, as seen through the eyes of Joel Sachs, whose story this is, we know them and their world of the Bronx so intimately that we care deeply about every one of them."
— Marilyn and Alan Bergman, Oscar-winning songwriters
   of "The Way We Were," "The Windmills of Your Mind,"
   and the score for "Yentl"

"I became so involved with Joel Sachs and his family, so caught up with the twists and turns of their lives, that I came to think of Joel as a secret family member of my own, who touched me so deeply that I felt bereft when his stories ended. Come back Joel!"
— Carol Kane, Actress in *Hester Street, Annie Hall, Taxi, Wicked*

Out of the Bronx

THE JOEL SACHS STORIES

JEROME KASS

A/V

ASAHINA & WALLACE

LOS ANGELES

2013

WWW.ASAHINAANDWALLACE.COM

CONTENTS

Published in the United States by Asahina & Wallace, Inc.
www.asahinaandwallace.com

Library of Congress Control Number: 2013956701

ISBN: 978-1-940412-06-1

For Delia
The love of my life

The Accident

On January 15, 1947, Joel Sachs celebrated his eighth birthday. Two days later he moved out of the bedroom he shared with his ten-year-old sister, Fanny, and started sleeping in the living room, separated by a pair of French doors from his parents' bedroom. This action came about because Fanny resented almost everything about him: he was "too nice"—a gentle boy with an easy-going temperament, their mother's declared favorite, adored by everyone in the family, pleasant to look at with his bright brown eyes and winning smile, an A student, always on the honor roll. Fanny was especially resentful because for his birthday, their parents gave him the bicycle, a bright red Schwinn two-wheeler, that she had been begging for since her ninth birthday and never received. She decided to get even with Joel once and for all, for everything he was and did that she wasn't and didn't.

Fanny was at best a C student. She was bitter, angry, competitive, combative, overweight, and generally miserable. Her sour disposition affected the way she looked. Feature for feature, she was actually very pretty, like her mother. Both had rosy red cheeks, voluptuous lips, chestnut brown hair, and deep, dark brown eyes. Her mother's hairdresser, Charles (Fanny referred to him as "Princess Charles" behind his back), would sigh whenever he saw Fanny and call her "Inga Borg," after Ingrid Bergman, whom he insisted Fanny resembled.

But it was hard for many people to tell how pretty Fanny was because her dark nature distorted her looks.

Her mother criticized her endlessly. Her father found her a constant disappointment. Grandma Sadie asked her regularly, "Why can't you be like your brother?" Whereas Joel's friends admired him, Fanny's girlfriends—or rather, girls who Fanny thought were her friends—called her a mean bitch behind her back. And her teachers always expressed dissatisfaction with her academic output and her conduct: "You could do a lot better, Fanny, if you focused on your schoolwork instead of your anger." Those like Mrs. Klein, Joel's third-grade teacher, who had taught Fanny before Joel, always remarked that he was a favorable contrast to his sister in every respect.

"You're nothing like her, thank goodness," Mrs. Klein told him.

On the night Joel moved out of the bedroom, Fanny was in an especially ugly mood because of that Schwinn bicycle she coveted. She tip-toed from her bed to his, which was not a long trek in this bedroom that was too small for two beds, leaned over so that her lips were almost touching his ear, and whispered, "Beware, Genevieve Polack"—the name she called him when she hated him—"tonight, when you're fast asleep, I'm going to stick hairpins into your eyes until they pop out and into your peepee until it falls off. Then I'm going to stand here laughing as I watch you die."

Although Joel was used to Fanny's cruelty, this particular threat to his cherished "peepee" made him cave. He started whimpering.

"That's right, Genevieve, cry. Cry like the little girl you are. But it won't do you any good when your blood is spilling all over your sheets and I flush your peepee down the toilet."

That was when Joel jumped out of his bed, called Fanny

"Monster!", and announced that he was moving out of their room for good. He grabbed his blanket and pillow, ran into the living room, and cried himself to sleep on the couch.

When his mother found him in the morning, she woke him and asked what he was doing there. He told her he couldn't share a room with Fanny anymore: she was too mean, and he couldn't take any more of her teasing. He begged his mother to let the couch be his bed from now on.

Rose immediately felt guilty. She knew it wasn't good for an eight-year-old boy to share a room with his ten-year-old sister, and she wished she and Lou could rent an apartment with a bedroom for each of the children. But Lou made only a modest living as a salesman in one of the neighborhood's two men's haberdasheries, and a two-bedroom was as much as he could afford. Rose took Joel in her arms and held him close, comforting him with her warmth and her heartbeat and her singular scent. Her eyes filled with tears, and she told him she was so sorry he didn't have a room to himself, but she would do what she could to make his life more pleasant. He hugged her and told her she was the most wonderful mother in the whole world.

Rose discussed the matter with Lou, who shrugged and said, "What's the big deal if he sleeps in the living room?"

So that became Joel's bedroom, leaving Fanny a bedroom to herself. Fanny was, of course, happier with this arrangement, although having a room of her own didn't stop her from teasing Joel relentlessly. It had become a way of life. Having moved out of the bedroom, however, Joel pretended not to hear her taunts, and without a reaction from him, Fanny lost interest, the teasing stopped, and the relationship between sister and brother relaxed.

As it turned out, Joel's sleeping so close to his parents'

bedroom proved to have a serious downside. French doors do not block sounds completely, and Joel was often kept awake by his parents' nightly bickering. Most of it was about money, how little they had and how hard it was to make ends meet. His mother always sounded angry, his father guilty. But on Joel's fourth night in the living room, the argument was only peripherally about money. The words were muffled at first, but what he could hear kept Joel not only wide awake, but on edge.

His father wanted something from his mother that she didn't want to give him, and he began to raise his voice insistently. His mother ordered him to lower it.

"Joel's in the next room," she reminded him sharply.

The next thing Joel heard sounded like whispered pleading from his father and hostile rejections from his mother. Joel didn't comprehend what the argument was about, but he could sense it was something serious and grown-up that he shouldn't be overhearing. His father kept begging, his mother kept refusing.

"Turn over and go to sleep already," his mother said.

"I'll give you an extra twenty-five this week," his father bargained.

"Not enough," she replied.

"How much is enough?"

"Fifty."

"Fifty? Are you crazy? You know I can't afford that kind of money."

Joel tried in vain to figure out what the transaction was about.

Then his mother said, "I won't spread my legs for less."

"Okay," said Joel's father, "fifty bucks it is. Spread."

For the next twenty minutes or so, communication between his parents was mostly grunts and groans. The only words were an occasional "Oh, baby!" or "You're the greatest" from his father, and from his mother "Are you through yet?" and "Stop sweating so much, you're sticking to me."

Joel didn't know why what he heard upset him, but he twisted and turned and covered his ears, trying to eliminate the sounds. Eventually, he heard a long moan from his mother and gasps from his father, which for a moment worried him. He thought one of them might be sick, maybe even dying. Then it occurred to him that what he was hearing might be his father beating his mother up. He couldn't believe his father was capable of beating anyone up, least of all his mother—the most beautiful, affectionate, loving human being on earth, as far as Joel was concerned. But then he remembered that about a year or so earlier, he had heard his father on the telephone cursing his own brother, Uncle Morris, calling him "a rotten shit" and other words Joel was never allowed to use. At one point, his father said that if he had a gun he'd come over and shoot Morris in the head. Joel had wondered for days if his father might be a murderer.

With that incident in mind, Joel worried for his mother's safety until he heard snores coming from the bedroom. His parents were fast asleep and all was right with the world—although Joel couldn't fall asleep until the sun was coming up. When he finally did sleep, he had a series of terrifying nightmares filled with monsters, madness, and murder.

The next night, much to Fanny's displeasure, Joel went back to sleeping in his own bed.

"What are you doing here?" she growled.

"I can sleep here if I want. It's my room, too," said Joel.

"You mean you're back for good?"

"Yes," he said. "It's not comfortable on the couch."

"I have no luck," she moaned.

Her teasing resumed, crueler than before, but Joel was impervious to it. After what he had heard that night in the living room, not even the worst of Fanny's vicious torments could impel him to sleep within earshot of his parents' bedroom again.

Some months later, as Rose served meatballs and spaghetti at the dinner table, Lou asked her a simple question that turned out to be not simple at all: "Did you see the doctor today?"

"Yes," said Rose, and it looked like she might break down and cry.

"The doctor?" asked Joel, alarmed.

Lou ignored him and said to Rose, "And?"

"And it's too late," said Rose, her hands trembling.

"Too late?" said Lou, in despair.

"Too late for what?" Joel asked.

"Butt out," Lou told Joel.

Rose bit her lower lip. "I'm almost in my fourth month."

"How come you went to the doctor, Ma?" asked Joel. "Are you sick?"

Rose said to Lou, "Can we discuss this later—when the you-know-who are not present?"

"Oh, don't mind us," said Fanny, sarcasm dripping from every word. "We're just your children. We don't count."

"If it's more money he wants," said Lou, "I'll find a way to give him an extra hundred."

"It has nothing to do with money," said Rose. "I don't want to discuss it now."

"Well, I do." Lou was insistent. He ordered Joel and Fanny to leave the table and go to their room.

Joel, baffled, stood up to leave, but Fanny wanted to hear

more. She grabbed Joel by the sleeve and pulled him back down into his chair.

"We're not finished eating," she said.

"I am," said Joel.

"No, you're not," threatened Fanny.

"Get out of here, I said," commanded Lou.

"But we're hungry," said Fanny.

"You'll live. Now, get going. Both of you."

"Go, children," said Rose, her voice shaky. "Do like Daddy says."

Reluctantly, Fanny took Joel by the hand and, with a grunt, led him out of the kitchen and into their bedroom.

"What's going on?" Joel asked, dazed.

"Mommy's pregnant," said Fanny.

"Pregnant?" said Joel, shocked. "You mean...?"

"Yes," snapped Fanny, furious. "We're going to have a damn brother or sister."

Joel was shocked. "How come?"

"How come?" Fanny repeated, incredulous. "Are you serious? Don't you know anything about sex?"

Joel shrugged. "I know some things."

Annoyed, Fanny explained. "Daddy got on top of Mommy and planted a seed in her vagina with his peepee, and the seed went to Mommy's belly, and out of the seed came a baby, and now it's growing inside Mommy, and when it's ready to be born, it'll slide out of Mommy's vagina."

Joel listened carefully and tried to understand. He also tried not to vomit. Fanny's graphic description made him sick to his stomach.

"Where does the seed come from?" he asked.

"I told you: from Daddy's peepee."

"You mean he pees into Mommy?"

"Sort of. When you grow up, your peepee will be able to get long and hard, and you'll be able to plant seeds too."

"My peepee gets hard sometimes."

"Well, good for you, but you're too young to have seeds in it."

"Oh." Joel was disappointed.

"Daddy's upset because it's too late for Mommy to have an abortion," Fanny continued.

"A what?"

Fanny couldn't believe her ears. "Don't tell me you don't know what an abortion is!"

Joel was embarrassed not to know things he apparently should know, but what could he do? "I'm sorry," he said.

"God! How can you be so stupid and still be breathing? An abortion is when they go into a woman's vagina and take the baby out of her. Only the baby isn't ready to come out yet, so it dies."

Joel squealed. "*Dies*? You mean Mommy and Daddy want the baby to *die*?"

"Face it," said Fanny dramatically, "they're murderers."

"But they didn't do it," Joel protested. "Mommy said it's too late."

"Well, they *thought* about doing it, and that's just as bad."

Joel's head was spinning. "How come Daddy doesn't want it if he planted the seed?"

"Don't ask *me*," she said. "Ask *him*."

"Me?"

"Well, you're the one who wants to know."

"Never mind, I don't care that much," Joel replied, afraid that asking might anger Lou the way Uncle Morris had angered him. Joel could wind up with a beating, at the very least.

"Come on," said Fanny, pulling him up off the bed. "Let's find out."

"No, I'm scared," said Joel.

Fanny dragged Joel back to the kitchen. Rose was in tears, washing dishes. Lou wasn't there.

"Where's Daddy?" said Fanny. "Joel wants to ask him something."

"No, I don't," said Joel, nervous. "Forget about it."

"I don't know where he is," said Rose. "I think he went out."

Joel could see that his mother had been crying. "Are you okay, Ma?" he asked.

"I'm a little upset," said Rose.

"Because you're pregnant, right?" asked Fanny.

"Yes," said Rose. "It was an accident."

"What do you mean?" Joel asked.

"We didn't want another child. We didn't plan on it. We can't afford it," said Rose.

"It's too late for an abortion, right?" said Fanny.

Rose was startled. "How do you know that?"

"I was sitting right here," said Fanny.

"You know what an abortion is?"

"Sure," said Fanny. "I read a story about it in *True Confessions*, and you know what happened in the story? The wife got an abortion, and her husband divorced her."

Joel was stunned. He understood "divorce." One of his friends at school was a child of divorced parents, and he cried about it a lot.

"You mean like Stevie Gross?" he asked Fanny. The idea made him shudder.

"Keep out of this, numbskull," Fanny sneered. "Ignore him," she told her mother. "He doesn't understand anything about sex or anything."

"Stevie Gross is a boy in my class," Joel informed her. "His parents got divorced, and he hardly ever sees his father."

"Who said anything about divorce?" said Rose, pulling herself together. "Now, look, children. This is not your problem. It's between your father and me. You just forget about it."

"*Forget about it*?" said Fanny. "You have a baby inside you that you and Daddy are thinking of killing, and you're telling us to *forget about it*?"

"Maybe you and Daddy don't want *us* either," said Joel. "Maybe you wish we were never born."

"Maybe you'd like to kill *us*," Fanny added.

"Don't be silly," said Rose, exhausted. "We love both of you more than life itself. An accident is different. Now, no more talk. Go and play."

"Do you want me to help you with the dishes?" asked Joel, who often dried when his mother washed.

"Go and play, I said."

"You think we're in the mood to play now?" asked Fanny, annoyed.

"Then *don't* play. Do something else," said Rose. "Knock your head against the wall."

"Huh" said Joel. "You mean it?"

"Just leave me alone!" Rose pleaded. "Give me some peace."

"Why are you mad at *us*, Mommy?" Joel asked. "We didn't do anything."

"That's right," Fanny said. "We didn't tell you to get pregnant. We didn't tell you we don't want the baby—even though we don't."

"*I* do," said Joel.

"No, you don't," said Fanny. She took Joel's hand and pulled him out of the room.

Alone, Rose collapsed into a chair and wept.

In the bedroom, Joel asked Fanny, "So what are we gonna do?"

"Nothing. We're gonna forget about it like Mommy said."

"What about after it's born? Are you gonna tell it that it was an accident, and Daddy and Mommy wanted to abortion it?"

"Of course not," said Fanny. "Would you want anyone to tell that to you?"

"No," said Joel unequivocally.

"Well, I'm definitely not going to say a word about it. Ever," said Fanny. "I may be mean, but I'm not *that* mean."

"I'm never telling either," Joel said.

But from then on, and long after his younger sister was born, Joel had nightmares of slimy holes being invaded by the veiny, bony, long-nailed hands of a horrible monster and of dead unborn babies being snatched from the holes and flung into the garbage. A few times, the monster sat on the dead baby's belly until, like a balloon, it exploded. And once or twice the monster stomped on the baby until it flattened like a cartoon character.

During the following months, as Rose's stomach grew bigger and bigger, the arguments between Rose and Lou grew more and more frequent and fierce. Fanny was amazed to overhear her father ask her mother in a very aggressive tone, "Okay, tell me the truth: who's the real father of this kid?"

Fanny reported to Joel what she'd heard.

The information upset and confused him. "Who does he think the father is?"

"Some other man, I guess."

"But you told me *Daddy* planted his seed into Mommy."

"Maybe I was wrong. Daddy thinks someone else stuck his peepee into her."

This was too much for Joel. He refused to believe it.

Not long after that, Joel overheard his father tell his mother, "I have a good mind to walk out of here and never come back."

"So go," said Rose. "I'll get as much from Welfare as I get from you."

Joel wanted to cry out, "No, Daddy, don't go! Don't let him leave, Mommy!" But he kept quiet and trembled with worry.

Whether or not Rose really wished that Lou would leave, no one knew. But Lou never left, and the bitter arguments continued right to the end of Rose's pregnancy.

"Who is he?" Lou persisted in asking at least once a day.

And Rose always answered with some version of "He was the pain in the you-know-what I'm married to."

Lou didn't believe her.

Neither did Fanny.

Only Joel did.

One morning in November, Rose came into the children's bedroom at about 5:30 and woke Joel and Fanny by turning on the overhead light. She was wearing a coat that barely covered her enormous belly, and she was carrying a small suitcase.

Joel sat sharply up in bed. "What's wrong?" he asked.

"My water broke," said his mother.

Half asleep and totally unnerved, Joel asked, "What do you mean?" He pictured a flood somewhere in the apartment.

"The baby is ready to come out," his mother explained. "Daddy is taking me to the hospital. He'll let you know as soon as the baby is born."

"Are we going to keep it?" Joel asked.

"The baby?"

"Yes," said Joel.

"Of course we are," said his mother.

"Good," said Joel, relieved. "I hope it's a girl." He turned to Fanny. "Don't you hope it's a girl?"

Fanny didn't answer, but her face said it all. From the first mention of her mother's pregnancy, Fanny was miserable about having a new sibling. She was even more miserable now that the intruder was almost here.

"You two go back to sleep until the alarm rings," said Rose. "Fanny, you're in charge. Make sure Joel drinks his orange juice and eats his cereal."

"Can I hit him if he doesn't?" asked Fanny.

"Definitely not, no hitting," said her mother. "And make sure you get to school on time, and dress warm."

With that, she winced and groaned.

Joel suffered with her. "Does it hurt, Mommy?"

"I had a contraction, that's all. I better get to the hospital. I think this is gonna be a fast one. You took almost a whole day," she told Fanny. "You were easy," she told Joel. "This one's gonna be easy, too."

"Of course," Fanny said, "*I'm* the one who was difficult. Big surprise."

"I'll call you later, when you're home from school," said their mother. "Be good children."

She gave each of them a kiss and left the room, calling, "Let's go, Lou."

"What's a contraction?" Joel asked Fanny when his mother was gone.

"It's when the baby kicks because it's trying to come out."

"Did you ever have one?"

"You're an idiot, you know that?"

"Why? Because I don't know some things?"

"Because you don't know *anything*!" She turned her back to him and closed her eyes.

"Well, how do you know about contractions if you never had one?" Joel asked.

Fanny sniggered. "I'm a genius. Now shut up and go to sleep."

A few hours later, Gloria Selma Sachs was born. Lou showed up at school and told the principal he needed to see his children so he could tell them the good news. The principal congratulated him and sent a messenger to bring Fanny and Joel to the school lobby. When Lou told them they had a new baby sister, Joel was elated—a sister, his dream come true—but Fanny was glum. She asked what the baby's name was going to be.

"Gloria Selma," said Lou proudly.

Fanny shrieked. "Are you kidding me? *Gloria*? *Selma*? Those are the worst names I ever heard!"

"We're naming her Gloria for Grandma Sadie's mother, Gertie," said Lou, "and Selma for my grandmother, Sylvia."

"Yuck!" exclaimed Fanny.

Joel said, "Does that mean the contractions stopped?"

"Yes," said Lou, smiling. "Mommy is fine."

Fanny was perplexed and annoyed. "You sound like you're happy to have this baby."

"I didn't say I'm happy, did I?" said Lou. "All I'm saying is she's gorgeous. She has thick red hair the color of Manischewitz wine, and eyes like a blue sky."

"How can she have red hair?" asked Fanny. You and Mommy have brown hair, and so does Joel and so do I."

"Well, Mommy had a great-great grandmother who had red hair."

"What about blue eyes?" Fanny asked. "Nobody in this family has blue eyes."

"The same great-great grandmother had blue eyes. You won't believe how beautiful this baby is."

"Looks aren't that important," Fanny lied, jealous and angry. There was no way she could feel anything but bitterness over this "gorgeous" Manischewitz-haired, blue-eyed trespasser into what Fanny now decided had been a very happy family.

Joel, on the other hand, was ecstatic. "When can I see her?" he asked.

"Mommy's gonna call you on the phone after school. She'll tell you when you can come visit her in the hospital."

Lou left, and as brother and sister walked back to their classrooms, Fanny grunted. "First he wants her to have an abortion, then he says the little bitch is gorgeous. He's crazy, I swear."

"Isn't a person allowed to change his mind?" Joel asked. But he was confused, too.

"He's probably not even the father," said Fanny. "Red hair? Blue eyes?"

"Daddy said Grandma Sadie's grandmother…"

"He's full of it," said Fanny, cutting him off.

As they approached Fanny's classroom, Joel said, "You're the one who's full of it. You're just jealous that you're not the only girl in the family anymore."

"Drop dead," she said, and disappeared into the room.

Joel adored Gloria from the moment he saw her through the glass in the hospital nursery. And when Rose brought her home from the hospital, and he held the baby in his arms for the first time, he knew that he was going to love her more than anyone. She was not going to be another Fanny, but rather a sister who would be nice to him and love him back. He would protect her and nurture her and give her the love he feared she would not get from Rose and Lou. In fact, right from the start he assumed the role of surrogate parent. Whenever Gloria cried and his mother or father didn't respond immediately, Joel would go to her and comfort her with light strokes on her forehead, gentle words, and kisses on her cheeks. If her diaper was wet, and he noticed it before his parents, he would put her on his bed and change her. When she awakened during the night, crying or squealing for attention, and Lou shouted at her to "shut up and let me get some sleep!" Joel would lift her out of her bassinet and rock her until she fell back to sleep. He fed, bathed, diapered, and dressed her whenever he was home. He held her in his lap, his head against hers, and hummed to her while they listened to music.

As Gloria started to walk and talk, there were many times when Joel preferred to stay home with her than go out and play with his friends. He sang to her and danced her around the room, which made her giggle with glee. He took her for walks and entertained her for hours, building whole cities with her out of wooden blocks. When his father paid him for baby-sitting, he used the money to buy Gloria gifts of toys, or dolls, or clothes, or ice cream. All he had to do was look at her, and she'd smile the most heartfelt smile, which for him was the best reward.

Fanny, on the other hand, ignored Gloria, except when Gloria occasionally sought Fanny's attention by poking her or calling out to her. Fanny would shout at her to, "Keep it down or you'll wish you were never born."

Joel couldn't understand how Fanny could not like Gloria. "She's such a sweet kid," he said.

Fanny replied, "At least I don't pretend I'm her mother like you do," which Joel couldn't deny. He did sometimes forget he wasn't Gloria's parent, but he didn't see anything wrong with it. His own mother was inattentive to her youngest, and he was just trying to fill that gap.

Eventually, Rose and Lou moved Gloria from her crib in the living room to a small bed in their bedroom. She was a chubby little girl, but very beautiful. Everyone noticed and commented on her head of hair: the thickest, most unusual burgundy-colored hair, unlike any they had ever seen. It became more extraordinary the older she got. Her skin was pink and delicate and without blemish from her forehead to her toes, an exquisite contrast to her hair. And those sky blue eyes—how they sparkled.

When Gloria was about five, Lou began to take a serious fatherly interest in her, more than he had done with either of his other children. He listened with pleasure as she read to him, held flash cards to help with vocabulary, and shared peanut-butter-and-jelly sandwiches with her, bite for bite. He took her to Coney Island on several Saturdays, which he had never done with Fanny or Joel, and he didn't invite them along now. Every Sunday, he took her to the neighborhood deli for hot dogs and french fries, leaving the rest of the family behind. A few times, Joel and Fanny saw their father doubled over in laughter at something Gloria said. And several times, they saw Lou rubbing his nose with Gloria's like Eskimos.

Their mother, too, became suddenly attentive to Gloria. Something about her hair, the longer and thicker it grew, brought out a strong feeling in Rose. She would spend hours shampooing it, setting it in curlers, brushing it, styling it. She praised Gloria for her looks, her temperament, her intelligence, her sweetness. She coddled her, bragged about her to friends and neighbors. She began calling Gloria her "doll baby," her "love child," her "future movie star." She said over and over that Gloria was God's blessing to a mother, and she thanked Him for giving Gloria to her. Joel and Fanny noticed all of it.

These changes made Joel feel secure about his baby sister's permanence in the family, and more assured that she was Lou's child. He decided not to remember having heard Lou deny his paternity years before. Best of all, he saw that Gloria would have more than enough love to grow up happy.

For Fanny, of course, the love her parents showered on the "accident" was a powerful new cause for her own despair and jealousy. She wondered if her father had once loved her like that, had read with her, laughed with her, rubbed noses with her, and if her mother had washed and brushed her hair and lavished praise upon her, too. She had no memory of it, and if it had happened, there was hardly a trace of it any longer, which saddened her and darkened her spirit.

When Joel cooed to Fanny about how great it was that "Daddy and Mommy are being so wonderful to Gloria," Fanny slapped him in the face and said, "Go to hell, sissy." Joel was stung by the response, but he let it pass. It was just Fanny being Fanny.

One day when Gloria was almost six, Joel was babysitting her while their parents went to the movies. Fanny, now sixteen, came into the living room and saw her brother and sister eating pretzel sticks and watching *I Love Lucy*, laughing their heads off. Fanny walked over to the TV, shut it off, and before Joel or Gloria could protest, Fanny blurted out to Gloria, "I have news for you, little bitch: you were an accident."

Gloria had no idea what Fanny was talking about, but Joel was shocked. When he scolded Fanny—"You said we were never gonna tell her that"—Gloria knew that Fanny's accusation wasn't a good thing, and she started to cry.

"You swore," Joel whined.

"I changed my mind," said Fanny. "Can't a person change her mind?"

Before Joel could say more, Fanny turned and disappeared into her room.

Joel tried to pacify Gloria. "Don't pay any attention to Fanny," he said. "She's just jealous of you because you're so beautiful and so smart and so terrific."

Weeping, Gloria asked, "What does it mean? What's an accident'?"

"It doesn't mean anything. Ignore her."

But Gloria persisted. "I know it means something. Please tell me, Joelly."

"It has nothing to do with you," said Joel.

Suddenly stern, Gloria said, "Tell me what it means. I wanna know."

Joel relented. "It means you weren't wanted."

"But if I wasn't wanted, you and Mommy and Daddy wouldn't love me, would you?" asked Gloria.

"That's right," said Joel. "So forget about Fanny, and let's watch *Lucy* and have fun."

Gloria willingly agreed.

So it went for the next few years. Joel gave Gloria his treasured two-wheeler and taught her to ride. He helped her with schoolwork and walked her to school every morning on his way to his high school. He picked her up on the way home. He took her to tap dancing class and watched her through the studio window as she accomplished a new combination, giving encouraging nods every time she glanced his way. He even took her along to the movies sometimes when he went with his friends, ignoring their protests. Their devotion to each other never flagged.

Fanny paid less and less attention to Gloria except to remind her, whenever she received praise from anyone in the family, that she was an accident and that all the good looks in the world, and the greatest personality, and the biggest brain wouldn't change that. Sometimes, even in her late teens, when she was feeling especially angry, she would call Gloria "an accident" in public. "Come on, Accident," she might shout. "Stop lagging behind." Joel suffered when he heard that, and so did Gloria, but she never gave Fanny the satisfaction of knowing that it upset her. She never defended herself, or asked her parents if the rumor was true.

By the time of Gloria's sixteenth birthday, Joel was twenty-four, teaching high school English, and living on his own in Manhattan. Fanny was twenty-six and unhappily married to Harvey, a shoe salesman no one in the family could stand. To quote Lou, "He looks like garbage, he talks like garbage, he smells like garbage, he *is* garbage." Even Joel, who normally found something to like about everyone, didn't like anything about Harvey, and with good reason: Harvey was a relentless and ruthless tease, worse even than Fanny. Harvey never called anyone by his given name. He called Joel "fag" or "intellectual" or "wimpy" or "snot-nose" or "schmuck." He called Gloria "a tragic accident" or "a hard pill to swallow" or "Miss Bronx virgin." Rose and Lou he referred to always as "the *alter cockers*". And he had a slew of names for Fanny, among them "fatso," "piggy," "cock-tease," "bitch," and worse.

Fanny knew that Harvey was as unpleasant and unpopular as she was. But she had wanted to be a wife and have a child or two, and no one else had asked her to marry him. So when

Harvey proposed, Fanny said yes. Two years later, they had their first child, a girl, Natalie. Harvey called her "my mistake" or "the disappointment" or "the pain in my ass."

For her Sweet Sixteen party, Joel took Gloria to Bloomingdale's and bought her the dress of her choice—a baby blue cocktail number—heels to go with it, and a faux pearl choker, bracelet, and earrings that Gloria judged to be "the most beautiful *ensemble* I could ever have wished for."

After Bloomingdale's, he took her to a restaurant, where, during lunch, Gloria remarked that just the other day Fanny had asked her if she ever wondered whether or not Lou was her real father.

Joel almost choked on his hamburger. "She's still teasing you about that? My God, when is she going to grow up?"

"Sometimes I think she's crazy," said Gloria.

"She is," said Joel, furious. "And mean."

"I told her she wouldn't say dumb things like that if she wasn't jealous of me. I said, 'Maybe if you weren't so mean, Mommy and Daddy and Joel would love you as much as they love me.'"

"You're so right," said Joel.

"She didn't think so," said Gloria.

After Natalie was born, Joel and Fanny met once a month at the Carnegie Delicatessen for brunch. Meeting monthly had been Fanny's idea. She surprised herself and Joel when she phoned him one day to say that it seemed to her they didn't see enough of one another, and she didn't want to lose their connection.

"Are you telling me you *love* me, Fanny?" Joel had asked, teasing her a little, but also wary of her motive.

"*Like*," said Fanny "I *like* you. Don't let's get carried away."

Joel laughed, tickled by Fanny's confession—and not too surprised. Despite all her hostility, Joel and Fanny had formed some kind of sibling bond based on many years of shared experiences and the compassion Joel felt for his older sister. The longer he knew her, the more he sensed her loneliness and isolation. He knew her marriage to Harvey was a sad mistake and that Fanny was not a happy wife.

"*Like* is good enough for me," he said.

The Carnegie Deli get-togethers mostly involved Joel listening to Fanny justify the anger and cynicism that had always defined her, telling him what he already knew: she trusted no one, she couldn't stand her husband, she didn't feel loved by Lou and Rose, she had no close friends, and on and on. It pained him that Fanny was so unhappy, and he offered encouragement when he could, always in an attempt to help her find some joy in life.

"What about your daughter?"

Fanny grunted.

"You always said you wanted a child."

"I was wrong," she answered. "All she does is pee and poop and eat. And she looks like Harvey. Maybe when she gets a little older I'll feel different."

"What about dancing?" Joel asked. "You used to love to dance. You taught *me* how to dance."

"Harvey doesn't dance. He has two left feet."

And so it went—an endless litany of complaints over the months of brunches.

One Sunday, Joel was on his way to the Carnegie to meet Fanny. It was a warm spring day, and he was early, so he decided to walk through Central Park. It was crowded with strolling humanity, and the roads through the park were blocked from traffic. Joel was tempted to buy a soft pretzel from one of the vendors, but he didn't want to spoil his appetite for brunch, so he continued on, listening to the songs of the birds, observing the many young women who passed, and thinking about sex, which he hadn't had for a while and sorely missed.

Suddenly, he stopped short, uncertain that he was seeing clearly. The equivalent of about half a block away from where he stood, on a bench under a tree, sat a woman and a man kissing. What struck him first was the man's thick head of Manischewitz-red hair, remarkably like Gloria's, although at this distance and with the sun spotlighting it, he wasn't sure that his perception of the color was accurate. The kiss ended, and now Joel could see the faces more clearly. The man was about forty-five and extremely handsome. The woman was Rose, now fifty-five. She smiled at the man and ran her fingers through his plentiful hair. The man gripped Rose's unoccupied hand, brought it to his lips, and kissed it with passion. Joel turned and walked quickly out of the park and towards the Carnegie, devastated to think his father had been right all those years ago. His mother was a cheater, and the man might be Gloria's father. Was it possible that his adored Gloria was not his full sister? No, he told himself. Positively not.

He was reeling as he entered the Carnegie. Then he heard Fanny call, "Joel! Over here!" and he made his way in a blur to Fanny's table.

"You're late," she said.

"Sorry," said Joel. "I got detained." He sat down.

"No kiss?" said Fanny.

Joel, upset, leaned over and pecked her on the cheek.

"What's wrong?" Fanny asked.

"What do you mean?"

"You seem distracted."

For a few moments, Joel didn't answer. He wasn't sure what to say.

"For crying out loud," said Fanny, "what is it? Are you sick?"

"No," said Joel. "Not the way you mean."

"Then what? Something's wrong and I want to know what it is."

A waiter came over to ask if they were ready to order.

"Not yet," said Fanny. "For God's sake, he just got here!"

"All right, take it easy, lady, I'll come back," said the waiter.

Fanny leaned in to Joel and asked, "So? What's the story?"

Joel thought about whether or not to tell her. A secret to Fanny was not something sacred. He well knew that she couldn't be trusted to keep it to herself. Hadn't she proved that when she told Gloria about being an accident?

Fanny seemed to read his mind because the next thing she said was, "If it's some kind of secret—I mean, if it's something you don't want me to tell, I promise I won't."

"I think I saw something I didn't want to see," Joel said, "but I'm not sure. That's all I'll say."

"What was it?" It was clear to Fanny that it was something important.

"The last time we shared a secret, you promised not to tell, but you did."

"That was a long time ago," said Fanny.

"How do I know that sometime in a fit of anger or jealousy you won't blurt this one out the way you did last time?"

"Because I said I won't, and I won't."

Joel wanted to believe her. He was bursting to reveal to Fanny what he'd seen. After all, who more than she would appreciate the gravity of the revelation?

"Please tell me, Joel."

Joel considered for a long time while Fanny sat and waited impatiently for his news. Should he or shouldn't he tell her? Would he live to regret it? Would Fanny betray his trust? Would she confront their mother with Joel's secret, or reveal it to their father or, worst of all, to Gloria? Finally, he made his decision.

"No," he said.

"You're not going to tell me?"

"Right," he answered.

"Really?" she said, genuinely surprised.

"Yes."

"You're sure?"

"Yes."

"Then fuck you!" said Fanny. She got up and walked off to the exit of the restaurant. As she was about to leave, she turned and gave Joel the finger. Then she disappeared.

Joel felt terrible. But he was sure he'd done the right thing. Whether he was right or wrong about the question of Gloria's paternity, he was determined to keep it locked up inside him for the rest of his life.

And he almost managed to do so.

The Bank

In the Sachs family, money ruled. Not that they were a wealthy family. Far from it. Rose regularly complained that Lou earned barely enough as a salesman in a neighborhood men's clothing store to support his family. He might have been able to do better for them, even with his modest income, if he weren't a gambler. After he gave Rose and the children minimal allowances on Friday night when he was paid, he lost much of the rest of his income on the trotters at Roosevelt Raceway on Long Island, or more recently at a new raceway in Yonkers. Or he lost it at poker or gin rummy or pinochle or *klabiash*. His cronies agreed that it wasn't simply bad luck: Lou, they said, was a lousy gambler.

Because he was usually a loser, he had to borrow a lot of money. When his relatives and friends, with a good deal of resentment for the un-repaid loans they had already made, refused to lend him any more, Lou went to "professional" money lenders whose interest demands were inhuman. Debts grew enormously with each day that passed, and after a short time, the money lenders would become impatient and make Lou's life a kind of hell. They'd call him several times a day, or appear at the haberdashery and confront him with vicious threats, often in front of customers and fellow salesmen.

"You like having two arms? How about two legs? You like them attached to your body?"

One night, Rose was out playing mahjong, and Lou was gambling at Yonkers Raceway. Fourteen-year-old Fanny was babysitting at an upstairs neighbor's, and Gloria, the four-year-old, was fast asleep in her parents' bedroom. Twelve-year-old Joel was alone in the living room, laughing at a skit with Sid Caesar and Imogene Coca on the fuzzy, twelve-inch Emerson TV screen, when the doorbell rang. Joel, still laughing, opened the door to a thug-like stranger, who asked gruffly, "Where's Lou?"

Joel's laughter ended instantly. "He's not here."

"You sure?" asked the stranger, pointing his index finger threateningly at Joel.

"Huh?" said Joel, surprised to be doubted. "Sure, I'm sure."

"Well, where is he?"

"I don't know."

The thug pointed his finger at Joel again. "You sure?"

"Look, I know when my father's here and not here, but I don't always know where he is when he's not here."

This time the thug made a fist and shook it close to Joel's face. "Well, tell him Mike was here. Tell him Mike said if he doesn't pay up by the weekend, he's in big trouble."

Mike turned and walked away.

Joel panicked. He called to Mike. "Pay up *what*?"

Mike didn't answer. He reached the staircase and started down.

"Money?" called Joel.

Mike disappeared.

"What are you gonna do to him?"

Silence.

Joel was terrified. He went into the small room he shared with his older sister, got into bed, trembling, and waited for Fanny to come home. When she did, he told her what had happened. To which she replied, "Well, he's a gambler. Of course, he owes money. That's what gambling is: you bet, you lose, you owe."

"But the man said Daddy will be in trouble if he doesn't pay up," said Joel.

"It's *Daddy's* problem, not *yours*," said Fanny. "He's used to it." She went into the bathroom to change into her bedclothes.

"Is the man gonna hurt Daddy?" Joel called to her.

"Probably," she answered.

When she returned, Joel asked, "Aren't you worried about him?"

"Not in the least," said Fanny. She got into bed, turned her back to Joel, and went to sleep.

Joel remained wide awake. His father came home about midnight. Joel got out of bed and found him in the kitchen, his arms and legs attached to his body, having a glass of milk. "A man was here looking for you," Joel told him.

Lou was immediately suspicious. "What man?" It was an attack more than a question.

"Mike," said Joel.

Lou started. "You opened the door?" he growled.

"Sure," said Joel. "Why wouldn't I?"

"Was it somebody you knew? Did you ever see him before in your life?"

"No," said Joel. "But I didn't know that until I opened the door."

"Why didn't you ask who it was?"

"I never hear *you* ask it before you open the door."

"All right. Never mind. Forget it," said Lou, irritated and defeated.

Joel was anxious. "Are you mad at me?"

"No," said Lou. "You're a good boy. Just don't open the door to strangers anymore."

"Is Mike a bad guy?"

"*I'm* the bad guy."

"How come?" Joel asked.

"Go to sleep," said his father.

"Is Mike gonna hurt you?"

"Go to sleep, I said."

The frequent fights between Joel's parents were usually about money. Lou didn't give her enough to live on except when he won at the races or cards, which was rare. When he lost—a more familiar occurrence—he reduced Rose's allowance sometimes to such a small amount that she couldn't afford to buy sufficient food for the week. When she railed at him for not being able to feed his family, Lou told her to get a job and help him out a little instead of *kvetching*.

"I should work to help you pay your gambling debts?" she asked.

"Do me a favor and just be quiet."

She obeyed. She tried to antagonize him as little as possible, knowing that otherwise he would start in calling her a whore, accusing her of having conceived their youngest child, Gloria, with another man.

Lou became so erratic about giving his kids their meager allowance that Fanny went out and got a job at Greta's Stocking Store, earning seven dollars for sweeping the floors and cleaning the dressing rooms and toilet every Thursday and Friday after school and all day Saturday. Joel got a job on Saturdays and Sundays as a delivery boy for Klinger's, the corner grocery. He earned two dollars, sometimes three, in tips, from which he gave Gloria ten cents, which had been her allowance before Lou canceled it altogether.

Fanny hated her job. She blamed her father for the "disgusting" work she had to do, and for her misery in general, because he gambled away her allowance. Joel worked hard for his two or three dollars, which, less the ten cents for Gloria, Rose "borrowed" from him whenever she "couldn't make ends meet," which was just about every week. Joel never refused her, even though he knew she couldn't repay him, and it hurt him to part with his hard-earned money that he had hoped to save and use towards his college education. But he couldn't refuse Rose anything. He believed it was his responsibility to be good to her to insure that she'd be good to Gloria.

Rose went to the beauty parlor once a week without fail, paid for by Joel's loans to her. Lou complained about her wasting money on "luxuries like the beauty parlor," but Rose defended herself adamantly. "The beauty parlor is my one indulgence," she would tell him, "and it's very important to me. I'm never going to give it up, no matter how poor we get." Rose's second indulgence, which she insisted was a necessity and also refused to give up, was a cleaning lady, Clara, who cost two dollars for a day's work once a week. Lou was fond of Clara and he liked how clean the apartment was after she left, but he resented the expenditure. "Two dollars for the colored girl is more than we can afford, Rose," he told her over and over.

"Oh, I see," Rose would reply sarcastically. "Two dollars for Clara we can't afford, but your gambling we can?"

"My mother never had a cleaning lady," said Lou. "My mother did her own cleaning until the day she died."

"Look, Lou," Rose repeated often, "I'll cook, I'll wash clothes, I'll go shopping, I'll do all the crap a wife's expected to do. But I won't clean, period. I'm not good at it. Even my mother—may she rest in peace—would never let me help her clean because she said I was the worst cleaner she ever saw.

A pile of crap could be laying on the carpet, and I wouldn't notice it."

Getting nowhere with Rose, Lou began to harass Fanny.

"If *you* would clean the house, we wouldn't have to throw away two dollars a week on a cleaning lady."

"You have to be kidding," Fanny told him. "I clean Greta's stinking store—including the *toilet*—three days a week. If you think I'm cleaning *this* place too, you've got another think coming."

"Okay, so don't clean," said Lou. "But at least pay for Clara."

"Hey, look," Fanny said, "I give you three dollars a week from my salary. I don't care how you spend it. If you want to use it to pay Clara, be my guest. But don't expect any more of my earnings."

If Lou complained endlessly about Rose's extravagances, Rose complained equally about Lou's gambling. In both cases, complaints were hopeless. Each was an addict of a kind, and they depended upon Joel and Fanny to pay for their addictions. Lou told Fanny over and over that he needed "just one extra dollar a week" from her, but she flatly refused to give it to him. He bullied her, he guilted her, he threatened her, but nothing worked. Fanny was indomitable, probably the toughest member of the Sachs family. Rose often said she wished she could have had two Joels or two Glorias instead of what God had given her in one Fanny.

On Joel's twelfth birthday, Lou came home with a big surprise: a bank. Not a conventional child's bank in the shape of a pig or made from glass or clay. No, this was a barrel made of wood, about three feet high, with a money slot big enough for dollar bills. Lou had built it for Joel with his own two hands.

Fanny said, "My God, it's so big! It'll never fit in our bedroom. Joel and I can hardly move in there as it is."

Lou said, "We'll make it fit. We'll rearrange the room."

"Why'd you make it so big?" Fanny asked.

"Because if Joel fills it up, he'll have a lot of money by the time he goes to college."

Lou told Joel to take a dollar of his earnings each week and deposit it in his new bank.

"But I always give Mommy all the money I earn," Joel said, "except for the dime I give Gloria. I don't have anything left over."

"Give Mommy one dollar less each week, and put it in the bank."

Rose was outraged. "Are you out of your mind, Lou? I *need* that dollar."

Lou ignored her. "Let's get the bank into your room."

"This I've gotta see!" said Fanny with a sneer.

Joel was excited as he helped Lou carry the bank. Rose followed. She told Lou it was very nice of him to do this for Joelly, "but the dollar should come from *you*, not from *me*."

With a gesture, Lou, brushed her off.

She didn't push any further.

Joel thanked his father profusely. "To tell you the truth," he said, "I've been wishing I could put something away for college."

"Well, now you'll have a dollar a week," said Lou magnanimously, as if it was *his* dollar and he was sacrificing it to his son. "And," Lou added, "the great thing is that there's no way to get the money out of the bank except to break it in pieces."

That surprised Joel.

"So no one will be able to steal your money," Lou added.

"You mean *my* money," said Rose with a grunt.

In order to fit the bank into the room, Lou replaced the desk chair with it. "There," he said. "The bank will be your chair."

Oh, great!" said Fanny and rolled her eyes. "An armless and backless desk chair!"

"Can I have a bank like that too, Daddy?" asked Gloria.

"Definitely," said Lou. "Someday."

"What about me?" asked Fanny.

"Not you," said Lou. "You don't deserve it."

"What if *I* want to go to college?" she asked in a jealous rage. "Joel gets everything. I get nothing."

"You have money," said Lou. "You only give us three dollars of it. If you want to go to college, buy yourself a bank and save the rest."

"I don't want to *save* it," said Fanny. "I want to *spend* it."

"Then forget about college," said Lou.

"Anyway," said Rose, "it's Joel's birthday, not yours. This is *his* present. You'll get *your* present when it's *your* birthday."

"Yeah," said Fanny sarcastically, "you'll probably buy *my* present with *my* three dollars!"

"You want a slap?" Rose asked.

"You're lucky I let you live here altogether," said Lou.

So Joel had a handsome new bank, which he loved. On Sunday, when he was finished at Klinger's, he ran home, excited, and put his first dollar into the bank. Feeling very successful, he called Gloria to his room and told her he wanted to play school. Gloria loved playing school with Joel as her teacher—not that she understood much of what he taught her. Using the barrel bank as his pretend teacher's seat, he sat down, adjusted his body to it in such a way that he was less uncomfortable, and looked around at his classroom of students, imaginary except for Gloria.

"Today I'm going to talk to you a little about Adolf Hitler."

"Oh, goodie," said Gloria, as if she knew who Adolf Hitler was.

"I'll start by reading to you from our history book. Listen closely because there will be a quiz tomorrow."

This was in fact Joel's own assignment for class tomorrow. With this game of pretend, he accomplished two things: he prepared for tomorrow's quiz and had fun acting out his fantasy of being a teacher.

A few days later, Clara was cleaning Joel and Fanny's room when Joel walked in, home from school. Joel adored Clara, and she adored him. She'd been the family's cleaning lady since before Joel was born. Everyone in the family loved her—except maybe Fanny, who insisted Clara lost a lot of her underwear when she washed the clothes at the neighborhood launderette. Rose considered Clara a friend as well as an employee, and would always prepare lunch for the two of them to eat together. They would gossip and laugh over lunch for more than an hour. Clara knew everything about the Sachses as told by Rose, and Rose knew as much about Clara's life as Clara was willing to reveal, which wasn't much, because she considered Rose way above her and was ashamed of her own lower-class life.

Today, when Joel walked into his room, Clara was dusting the new bank.

"Joel," she asked, "what is this?"

"It's a bank," said Joel. "You see? The money goes in here," and he demonstrated for her by tearing a piece of paper about the size of a dollar bill from his loose-leaf notebook. "Pretend this is a dollar," he told Clara. He folded it in thirds and deposited it into the bank.

"That's just fine," said Clara.

"My father made it," Joel said with pride, "with his own two hands."

"And where's the money gonna come from that's supposed to be goin' in this here bank?" she asked. "I'm talkin' *real* money, not scrap paper."

Joel explained his plan to save a dollar a week from the money he made at Klinger's.

"And what're you goin' to do with all the money you save?" she asked, impressed.

"It's for when I go to college."

Clara smiled and nodded. "You're a fine boy, Joel." She embraced him and kissed him on the cheek. Joel kissed her cheek in response.

Fanny saw them exchanging kisses as she walked in, home from school. "What are you two lovebirds up to?" she asked.

Clara laughed and said, "We was just admiring this here bank."

"Oh," sneered Fanny, still resentful, "that *bank*! By the way, Clara," she said smugly, changing the subject, "Would you happen to know where I could find my orange panties with the balloons on them?"

"Ain't they in the drawer?" asked Clara. As an afterthought she added, "Ain't your *draws* in your *drawers*?" and she and Joel laughed at her pun. Fanny did not.

"I hope you'll make an effort to find them, Clara," Fanny said. "I mean, we don't pay you to lose my clothes."

Fanny's rudeness pained Joel. If it had been directed at him, he'd have ignored it, but he felt protective of Clara. "Can't you show Clara some respect, Fanny?" he asked.

"Oh, she don't need to be nice to me, Joel," Clara said. "I got better people than her showin' me respect. Like *you*, for instance."

"As usual," said Fanny, "I do everything wrong, he does everything right."

Over the following weeks, Joel never neglected, on any Saturday or Sunday when he came home from work with tips, to feed the bank a dollar bill. On a page of his loose-leaf notebook, he kept an accounting. According to his records, twelve weeks had passed since his birthday, so there were twelve one-dollar bills in the bank. In two days it would be the weekend, and on Saturday, he'd be depositing his thirteenth dollar. He was very proud of himself, and his pride served him well, because that Saturday he came home with two dollars in tips, double his usual daily earnings. His good nature and high spirits that day had apparently affected his customers. Many of them tipped him more than usual—thirty-five cents instead of twenty-five in several cases, and even one tip for forty cents.

As he passed through the kitchen, where his mother was preparing dinner, he beamed. "Thirteen dollars coming up!" he announced with fanfare. He handed Gloria her dime and his mother ninety cents and went directly to his room with the other dollar.

"I made more than usual today, Ma," he called back.

"Not me," said Rose, still depressed to have sacrificed that dollar each week.

Joel entered his room, and what he saw made him stop short. He blinked his eyes several times to be certain he was seeing what he was seeing. His bank had been completely demolished. There were chunks of wood all over the floor and desk and beds. And no money to be seen anywhere.

His heart skipped a beat. Then came one quick beat after another. He thought he was having a heart attack. A news bulletin flashed through his mind: "Twelve-year-old Joel Sachs, the youngest boy in history to have a heart attack." He stared at the broken bank and shrieked. Rose and Gloria came running into his room. Both were shaking.

"What?" asked Rose.

"Look!" Joel cried.

Rose and Gloria saw the devastation. Rose gulped. "Oh, my God!"

Gloria started to cry.

"Who would do a thing like that?" asked Joel.

"I can't imagine," said Rose. To Gloria, she said, "Crying doesn't help anything."

"It helps *me*," said Gloria.

"Robbers?" asked Joel.

"Clara came in for a few hours today to do some ironing she didn't get to on Tuesday," said Rose.

"Clara?" Joel echoed. "Are you accusing Clara?"

"Don't be silly," said Rose, "Clara would never do anything like this. Clara loves you."

Joel wept. "Who would do it?"

Gloria said, "I'm trying to stop crying, Joel, but if you cry, I have to cry, too."

Joel stopped crying.

"How much was in it?" Rose asked.

"Twelve dollars." He wanted to sob and stomp the floor with his feet, but he controlled himself for Gloria's sake.

Rose began rubbing her hands over and around each other in a state of acute anxiety. She dreaded saying what she said next.

"Fanny?"

"Fanny?" Joel was surprised.

"She's capable of it," said Rose.

"Fanny would never do anything like that. I know she can be mean, *very* mean…"

"A mean, jealous bitch," said Rose. "Let's be honest."

"But I really don't believe she'd do that to my bank."

"I hope to God you're right," said Rose, "because if I find out it was her, I'll throw her out into the street, and she can live there for the rest of her life."

She went back into the kitchen.

Joel studied the smashed barrel, trying desperately to understand who would do such a thing. Why would they, whoever they were, destroy something that a father had built with his own two hands and given as a gift of love to his only son? How could it be Clara, who was virtually a member of the family? How could it be Fanny, who was his flesh and blood? He lay down on his bed and stared at the ceiling, searching his mind for an answer.

Gloria stood on tiptoes and gave Joel a peck on the cheek.

He smiled sadly and thanked her. "I'd like to be by myself for a while, Gloria."

"Okay," said Gloria. "Call me if you need me." She turned and left the room, heartbroken for her brother.

A few minutes later Fanny was home from work. As she passed through the kitchen, Rose, without even a hello, asked, "Was it you?"

Fanny stopped short. "Huh?" she asked. "Was *what* me?"

"Take a look in your room," said Rose.

Puzzled, Fanny walked into the room and was thrown by what she saw.

"Who did that?" she asked Joel.

From the bed, Joel answered, "That's what I'm trying to figure out."

Fanny remembered her mother's accusatory question.

Furious, she returned to the kitchen. "You think *I* did that?" she asked Rose.

"Did you?" Rose asked again.

"Are you nuts?" Fanny asked. "*When* did I do it? Was I even home today? Do you think so little of me that you think I would do something like that?"

"I don't think you did it," said Rose. "I'm just asking to be sure."

"Well, you can be sure you insulted me—thank you very much. I'm glad to know I've been right my whole life about one thing: you don't love me."

"Don't be silly," said Rose. "Of course I love you. But sometimes even people you love do bad things."

"You never loved me." Fanny turned in a huff and marched into the room she unhappily shared with her brother. She looked daggers at Joel, lying there on his small bed and said, "I suppose *you* think it was me too, huh?"

"Look, Fanny," Joel pleaded, "I'm very upset, and I'm not in the mood to fight. So if you didn't do it, then I'm glad, and I believe you, and I don't want to discuss it."

"Oh, really?" countered Fanny. "*I'm* the one who gets accused of being a criminal, and *you* don't feel like discussing it!" She plopped down on her bed, deeply upset. "I hate this family!" she muttered. "And to tell you the truth, I hated that bank. It took up half the room and it was uncomfortable to sit on."

"The money was gonna be for college."

"How much was in it?"

"Twelve dollars."

"Twelve dollars for *college*?"

"It may not seem like much, but it was the first twelve dollars I ever saved," said Joel, "and it was only the beginning."

"Well, I'm not saying it's not a yucky thing somebody did,"

said Fanny, "but at least it was only twelve dollars they got."

Joel lay there feeling sadder than he could ever remember. Destroying a gift that his father had given him and stealing money that he had worked so hard to accumulate seemed to him as bad a thing as anyone could possibly do.

Fanny played a recording on the phonograph of Dinah Shore singing "Buttons and Bows." She played it loud.

"Could you please turn it down?" Joel asked.

Fanny looked at him as if he were a moron. "I'm purposely playing it loud to make you feel better!" she said.

"Thank you," said Joel, "but it's not working."

Fanny left the record playing at the same volume. Then she said, apropos of nothing, perhaps to distract her brother from his gloom, "Marlene says *The Naked and the Dead* is very dirty. I bet she's only reading the dirty parts."

Joel begged Fanny to turn off the music. "I'm too depressed for Dinah Shore."

"Well," said Fanny, "you're not the only one who lives here," and she started dancing around the room to the music. The room was too small for movement of any kind and more difficult now with chunks of wood everywhere. Fanny compensated for it by dancing first on her bed, then on the desk, and then jumping onto Joel's bed, thrusting her foot in his face, ordering him to smell it.

Joel couldn't understand why Fanny didn't have enough sympathy to stop taunting him. After all, his *bank* had been destroyed and *twelve dollars* was gone. But there was no understanding Fanny. She was a total mystery to him.

Lou came home from work in time to sit down for dinner with the family. It always took Rose a long time to get food on the table because everyone ate a different meal. Fanny had spaghetti every night with a can of Campbell's Tomato

Soup poured over it. (Which, along with Lou's insistence that everyone eat bread with every meal, explained her chubbiness. "If you don't have bread with dinner, you aren't really eating, you're *noshing*," was Lou's mantra, and they all bought it, so they were all overweight.) Joel always had a lamb chop and mashed potatoes, some nights with string beans, other nights with spinach. Gloria had a scrambled egg. Lou, who had false teeth, three of them broken, ate six hamburgers every dinner, which didn't require a lot of difficult chewing. Rose prepared them from chopped chuck steak with eggs, matzo meal, onions, and lots of salt and pepper, and then fried them in Crisco—the only way Lou liked them. Rose ate everyone's leftovers. She would pile them all on one plate and have her dinner after everyone else had eaten their fill and left the table. Joel often questioned her about it.

"Why do you always eat leftovers? Why can't you make something of your own?"

Rose always replied, like a martyr, "I like bones."

Only for Friday night dinners did everyone agree to eat the same meal: roast chicken, boiled potatoes, boiled carrots, and boiled string beans, accompanied by *challah*. It was also the one night a week Rose had her own meal, the same as the others, and dumped her leftovers into the garbage along with everyone else's.

Nobody said anything to Lou about the broken bank until he noticed that Joel was staring at his food instead of eating it.

"What's with you, Joel?" he asked. "Why aren't you eating your lamb chop?"

Joel burst into tears.

Gloria, now also in tears, cried to her father, "The bank."

"What about it?" asked Lou.

"Somebody broke it and took the money," said Rose.

"What?" asked Lou. "Who would do such a thing?"

"We don't know."

Fanny said, "They think it was *me*."

"Was it?" asked Lou in the same matter-of-fact way her mother had asked.

"No!" Fanny thundered, more insulted than ever. "I'm not a thief!" To both parents she directed the question, "What kind of people are you? I'm your *daughter*, for God's sake! You should know me better than that. Don't you have any respect for me?"

Lou asked, "So if not you, who then?"

"Did you ever think of Clara?" asked Fanny.

"Once and for all," said Rose, "Clara would never steal from us. And she would never smash Joel's bank that way. Joel is like a son to her."

"Maybe she couldn't help herself," said Fanny. "Maybe she needed the money. She's poor, you know."

"She makes a good point," said Lou.

"It wasn't Clara," said Joel confidently.

"How do you know?" Fanny asked him.

"I just do."

Lou asked his wife, "Who was in the house today besides you and Clara?"

"Nobody," said Rose.

"Well," said Lou, "the bank didn't break itself. And the money didn't just disappear. It was you or Clara."

"It was not me, and it was not Clara," said Rose. "Clara was here only a couple of hours, and I went out shopping. Then there was nobody here."

"I have a feeling we'll never know who it was," said Joel. "But I think whoever did it is the worst person in the world."

"Not necessarily," said Fanny. "Not if the person had a good reason."

Rose said, "A good reason to steal from a twelve-year-old boy who happens to be the sweetest twelve-year-old boy in the whole United States of America?"

"That's *your* opinion," Fanny said.

"Ask anyone in the neighborhood, ask his teachers, ask his friends, ask Grandma Sadie," said Rose. "It's *everyone's* opinion."

"Not mine," said Fanny under her breath.

"You know something, Fanny?" said Rose. "With that nasty tongue, I'm beginning to think it *was* you that robbed your brother."

"That's because you hate me," said Fanny defensively. "Just like everyone else in this family."

"If it *was* you who took Joelly's money, you can be sure we'll all hate you," said Rose.

Fanny jumped up and shouted, "Dammit to hell, I didn't take the goddamn money!"

"Watch your mouth, young lady," warned Rose.

Fanny grumbled and ran into her room, slamming the door after her.

Joel said, "I believe her."

"You're too good-natured," said Lou.

After dinner, Gloria went to bed, and Rose, Lou, and Joel sat down in the living room to watch *The Honeymooners*. Fanny chose to be by herself in her room, still seething over the family insults. Rose and Lou loved Art Carney. Normally, Joel enjoyed the show too, but tonight he was depressed and couldn't focus on anything but the crime that had been perpetrated against him. When Rose brought a bowl of fruit from the kitchen and offered Joel an apple, he declined and asked to be excused.

"I'm going to bed." He went into his room.

Nobody tried to stop him.

Ignoring Fanny, who was sitting on her bed, clipping her toenails, Joel lay down on his bed to think about who could have done it.

In the living room, Rose said, "Poor kid."

"Shush!" Lou told her. "I'm trying to watch."

His response surprised Rose. She looked at her husband, who was engrossed in the TV show, and wondered how he could not feel for his own son—his wonderful boy who had been so hurt. How could a father just sit there and watch *television* and *laugh*?

In the middle of a very funny scene between Jackie Gleason and Art Carney, Rose got up and, without a word, turned off the TV.

Taken by surprise, Lou said, "What are you doing?"

Rose looked at him fiercely. "Did you break the bank and take the money, Lou?"

Lou looked at her stunned. "Am I hearing right?" he asked.

"Did you?" she repeated.

Breathless from the shock of the accusation, he asked, "You think I left work and snuck into my own son's room and broke a bank that I myself made for him with my own two hands and stole twelve dollars?"

"How do you know it was twelve dollars?" asked Rose.

"How do I know?" Lou said, a little flustered. "Joel said so."

"I didn't hear him," said Rose.

"I've been counting the weeks myself, and it added up to twelve."

Rose was silent.

"You really think I did that terrible thing?" Lou asked.

"Who else?" asked Rose.

"Why not Clara?"

Rose grew very serious. "You did it, Lou, didn't you?"

Lou started to respond. "I can't believe…!" Suddenly, he started to weep. After a moment, he said, "I owed a shylock. He threatened to hurt my family if I didn't pay up."

"Twelve dollars?" she asked.

"Forty," said Lou. "I borrowed the rest from another shylock."

Rose was silent for some time, trying to decide what she would do with this dreadful information.

She stared at her husband with angry eyes. "How am I gonna tell Joel that his father, who supposedly loves him so much that he made a bank for him with his own two hands, is also the thief who stole his money?"

"You have to tell him?" asked Lou, deeply ashamed.

Again, Rose was silent. She bit her lip, she rubbed her hands, she scratched her head, she dotted her damp forehead with the dish towel, and then, finally, she said, "I'm opening the window, and I'm letting the whole disgusting mess fly away forever. Gone and forgotten."

Lou watched her open the window and fan the crime out. He felt guilty and relieved. He got up, walked over to his wife, embraced her and kissed her in gratitude.

"You better stop the gambling," she said.

For Joel, the incident wouldn't go away. It was on his mind all day, every day, interfering with his academic performance and his conduct in class, with his friendships, and with all his other relationships. As he told his mother, "I've got to know who did it. I've got to know who the monster is that wrecked my bank and stole my twelve dollars."

Rose tried to make light of it. "Get over it already," she said. "It's probably better not to know."

But Joel couldn't let it go. The image of that broken bank had pierced his heart and left a big hole. And now it was taking over his brain. "I've got to know the truth," he told Rose over and over again. "It's driving me crazy!"

"It hurts my heart to see you like this, Joelly. It kills me."

On Tuesday, when Joel came home from school, he asked his mother where Clara was. "Isn't today her cleaning day?"

"I fired her, said Rose," her voice shaking.

"What?" said Joel. "*You fired Clara?*"

"She was the one who broke your bank and stole your money after all."

"Clara?" Joel was incredulous.

"I know," said Rose, "It's hard to believe. I was surprised too. But she confessed it to me."

"Clara?" he repeated.

"She said she felt terrible, but she needed the money."

Joel said nothing more to his mother. He called Gloria. "Come into my room, we'll play school," he said.

Gloria appeared and entered his room with him. He closed his door, and looked around in silence for a while. Gloria sat down on Joel's bed and made herself comfortable.

With a catch in his throat, Joel said to Gloria and his imaginary class, "I don't have my bank to sit on anymore, so from now on I'll have to stand when I'm teaching."

Joel Fresser, The Chocolate Virgin

By his fourteenth year, Joel Sachs had developed a serious chocolate addiction and gained a lot of weight. Until then, he was not what you would call thin, but now he was clearly fat. In fact, he was the fattest student in the freshman class at Bronx High School of Science, weighing a hundred and ninety pounds. He wasn't happy about it. When he stood naked before the mirror and saw the flab dripping from his youthful body, he felt like crying. He knew that chocolate was the cause of his obesity, but he could not give it up. His older sister, Fanny, called him "Fatty," although she herself was overweight. Joel would say something in response like, "What about you? I may eat a lot of chocolate, but you eat more spaghetti and potatoes than anybody in the world!"

Fanny would say, "Maybe so, but at least I'm pretty. You're ugly."

It wasn't true that Joel was ugly. In fact, he had a very nice face. But he accepted Fanny's judgment of his looks ever since his mother introduced him to a group of her mahjong girl-friends thus: "This is my Joelly. He's not good-looking, but he's so good." What fourteen-year-old boy cares about being *good*? It's being *good-looking* that matters. And if his mother didn't think he was good-looking, how could *he* think so?

Chocolate was Joel's weakness and his passion. He loved it in any form: candy, cake, cookies, ice cream, pudding, egg creams. His day began with a breakfast of hot cocoa and two, sometimes three, chocolate-covered doughnuts, Stuhmer's if possible, because Stuhmer's had a bittersweet chocolate frosting that made Joel tingle with pleasure. It ended at bedtime with a glass of chocolate milk and three or four Mallomars, chocolate-covered marshmallow domes on a thin vanilla wafer base. Between wake-up and bedtime, Joel stuffed himself with more chocolate. On his way to school in the morning, he stopped at Cohen's candy store to buy six or seven Nestlé's bars and add them to the sandwich and dessert (Oreos, with the cream center) in his lunch box as snacks during his classes. On his way home from school, he always stopped at Cohen's again for chocolate ice cream—a cone, a soda or a malted. Dessert after dinner was usually chocolate cake.

Chocolate was more than a food source to Joel. He was miserable because of what it did to his body, but at the same time it had what might be called a spiritual effect on him. It filled him with hope and joy and optimism. On a day when he would rather stay in bed than get up and go to school, he thought of all the chocolate that awaited him, and he arose with enthusiasm, dressed quickly, and rushed into the kitchen for his first fix of the day. When something bad happened to him and life looked grim—when he failed an exam or a teacher scolded him or Fanny was mean to him—he stuffed his face with something chocolate and the bad feelings went away. At night, after milk and cookies, he would get under the covers and—as quietly as possible so that Fanny in her nearby bed wouldn't hear—pleasure himself.

Joel was never sure when the need would grip him during class. When it did, he would sneak his chocolate provision out of his lunch box and wolf it down, unseen by the teacher. Part of the pleasure of the Nestlé's snack was the challenge he posed for himself of holding out as long as possible in each class before he succumbed to his craving. Occasionally, he managed to resist temptation until just before the class ended. At those times, the pleasure of the chocolate was very great indeed. But most of the time, his need overwhelmed him early on, and he couldn't restrain himself beyond ten minutes after a class started.

His mother, despite her own addiction to bread and butter, worried about Joel's chocolate consumption. The family doctor had urged her to get Joel to stop the sweets for fear he might wind up with diabetes. But no matter how much Rose pleaded with him to "stop *fressing* so much chocolate," Joel was helpless to obey.

His teachers and classmates were well aware of his obesity. His biology teacher more than once singled him out in a classroom of thirty-five students as an example of a person with the greatest future likelihood of cardiovascular disease, colitis, or diabetes, possibly all three. His classmates called him "Joel the chocolate mole," which upset him but had no effect on his habit. You don't cure addiction by humiliating the victim.

Supporting a chocolate habit like Joel's was not easy for a fourteen-year-old high school freshman with no job and only a two-dollar-a-week allowance. He'd worked for a time delivering groceries, but he'd quit when he discovered that the money he'd saved had been stolen by the cleaning woman from the bank his father had made for him. He saw no point in working if his hard-earned and hard-saved money was going to be stolen.

Over and over, he begged his father for an increase in his allowance. Lou always turned him down. Not because he was cheap—although he was. The bigger reason was that he was so deeply in debt to money lenders for his constant gambling losses that he could barely afford the two dollars he gave Joel each week.

So Joel had to find another way to satisfy his chocolate need on those occasions, which were frequent, when his purchasing power was extremely limited. He asked his mother for a dollar extra, but even if Rose had an extra dollar in her purse—which she rarely did—she told him that he didn't need more chocolate than she provided and, furthermore, if he wound up with diabetes, as the doctor had warned, he would have to sacrifice all sugar from his diet. But an addict is an addict. Threats don't work any better than humiliation, and Joel pleaded with Rose over and over for "just one more dollar a week."

"It hurts me more than you to turn you down, darling, but only a bad mother would help a wonderful son like you get diabetes, so don't ask me again because the answer will always be no."

Joel wasn't sure what to do, but it was clear he had to do something. He simply could not live without a sufficient supply of chocolate each day.

One night, as he was falling asleep, an idea occurred to him. He would pay Mr. Cohen, the candy store owner, for one or two Nestlé's bars but put four or five into his briefcase. It was not in Joel's nature to steal—especially when he remembered how much pain it had caused him to have his own savings stolen—but he was desperate. His need for chocolate was out of his control, so he had no alternative but to become a thief.

For a few weeks, he got away with it. But one morning on his way out of the candy store, Mr. Cohen stopped him and snatched his briefcase.

"I want to look through this," he said.

Joel began to tremble. "How come, Mr. Cohen?" he stammered.

Mr. Cohen brought his hand out of the briefcase holding five Nestlé's bars.

"You're stealing from me, Joel Sachs?" he said. "You, of all children? I'm very shocked and very disappointed."

Joel started to cry.

"How long has this been going on, young man?" asked Mr. Cohen. "Be honest with me."

In tears, Joel answered, "Just about a month, Mr. Cohen. That's all."

"That's *all*?" echoed Mrs. Cohen.

Cohen turned to his wife, who was watching with horror. "You believe this?" he asked her.

"His mother will die!" she exclaimed.

Joel begged, "Oh, please don't tell her, Mrs. Cohen! Please! I swear I'll make good for the candy."

"How?" asked Mr. Cohen. "Where will you get the money? You'll steal from somebody else?"

"No, never again," promised Joel. "I'll figure something out, I swear."

In the end, the Cohens did not report Joel's crime to his parents. Mrs. Cohen decided the shock might be too much for Rose Sachs.

That night, Joel was frantic. How was he ever going to pay the Cohens back? More important, where was he going to get the chocolate he needed to make it through the school day? He would still have his doughnuts and hot chocolate for breakfast, Oreos from his mother in his lunch box, chocolate cake or ice cream after dinner, and Mallomars and chocolate milk before bed. But what about the snacks he craved during each class or the ice cream after school? He lay awake the whole night feeling hopeless and very sorry for himself.

The next day at school was hell for him. His deprivation was so painful that during history class he began to moan. Mr. Pollack, the teacher, asked him what was wrong.

"My stomach hurts," whimpered Joel.

Mr. Pollack told him to go to the boys' room until he felt better.

In his English class, he failed a grammar quiz for the first time ever. During Phys. Ed., his archenemy, Jimmy Keegan, tripped him. Normally, Joel would have fought back. He could easily beat Jimmy up—Keegan was as thin as a rail, so all Joel had to do was sit on him. But today he felt so weak and depressed that he simply said, "I know you didn't mean it," and that was the end of it.

When school was over, Joel rushed home in a frenzy of need and searched the kitchen until he found a box of Hydrox cookies, an imitation of Oreos—not ideal, but good enough. He wolfed down the entire box like a hungry animal. His chocolate appetite was satisfied for the moment, but he was sure he couldn't survive another chocolate-less day of school.

He sank into a deep depression, and by four P.M. he climbed into bed in an attempt to relax and discovered that he couldn't get an erection. Normally, with the chocolate fix his body demanded, he would play with himself, and in no time he'd be hard as a rock. A minute or two later he'd explode and release what felt to him like a volcano. Less than a minute after that, he'd be peacefully asleep. Now, however, even without Fanny in the room, no matter how much he stroked and pulled, he remained soft. After an hour of tugging his sore, limp organ, he was panicked: if he couldn't have an orgasm at bedtime, he wouldn't be able to sleep. And what Joel craved most after his nighttime chocolate was sleep.

That evening he told his mother he was skipping dinner and going right to dessert.

"What are you talking about?" asked Rose.

"I had a very hard day in school today, and I'm too tired to eat. I just want my dessert and I'll go to sleep."

His mother was suspicious. This had never happened before. But she allowed that her angel of a son was tired from his schoolwork, so she gave him his dessert. When he was finished, she told him to go and get a good night's sleep.

"Where's Fanny?' he asked.

"She's sleeping at Annabelle's tonight."

"I thought Fanny and Annabelle had a fight."

"They made up."

"So you mean I'll have the room to myself tonight?"

"No," said Rose. "Gloria wants to sleep in Fanny's bed."

Joel couldn't hide his disappointment. "Oh."

"Are you happy that I'll be sharing your room, Joel?" asked Gloria, excited.

"Of course I'm happy," said Joel. "Eat your dinner. And try not to make any noise when you come into the room. I'll be asleep."

"I'll be very quiet," said Gloria.

Joel went into the bedroom, got undressed and into bed. He assumed after having had chocolate cake and a few Mallomars and without anyone else in the room to distract him that he'd have no problem satisfying himself and falling right to sleep. But that wasn't the case. Clearly, the chocolate snacks he didn't have in school were a serious loss, because he still couldn't get hot enough to get hard. This led him to panic, which of course exacerbated his sleeplessness, so he was wide awake when, an hour or so later, Gloria entered the room on tiptoes. She was already in her pajamas, and she got into Fanny's bed. In less than ten minutes she was fast asleep. Joel, however, was up all night. At about 6 A.M., he was at the window near his bed, watching his first sunrise and making an important decision: he would have to find a job.

In a state of total exhaustion in school that day, he considered what kind of work he might do. In the middle of geometry, he concluded that the job that suited him best, and might even be somewhat enjoyable, was candy-store work. Not only would such a job provide him with money with which to pay back the Cohens, but he would also be surrounded by as much chocolate as he needed.

He envisioned himself behind a counter, covered by a white ankle-length apron, the kind Mr. Cohen wore—scooping ball after ball of smooth, rich chocolate ice cream, ladling out thick oozing hot fudge, mixing egg creams, shaking malteds, and preparing sundaes, and serving everything with joy and gusto to a candy-store public that would respond with heartfelt *oohs* and *aahs*. In this fantasy, Joel became the neighborhood hero.

In Spanish class he began to daydream about all the chocolate concoctions he would invent, testing them first on himself, and then, if they met his high standards, introducing them to customers. He imagined a chocolate malted made with two inches of chocolate syrup, four scoops of chocolate ice cream, a tablespoon of malt, and a Nestlé's bar that he would break into pieces at the bottom of the glass like the prize in a box of Cracker Jacks. He saw dozens of customers lined up outside the candy store, desperate to be served one of the notorious creations of Joel Sachs, "the greatest counterman in the Bronx."

Right after school, Joel went job hunting.

Cohen's was the most popular candy store in the

neighborhood, with the largest and most varied stock. It was closest to Joel's apartment house, so it would be the most convenient place for him to work. But of course, he couldn't apply for work where he was regarded as a criminal. So he walked three blocks further to the next candy store, a tiny storefront, which, like its owner and sole operator, Mrs. Katz, was old, run-down, and unpopular.

Mrs. Katz was a childless widow, who for the past five years since her husband died had run her store alone. Being an elderly woman on her own in a neighborhood that had its share of thefts and other crimes, Mrs. Katz was suspicious of almost anyone who entered the premises. To her, children especially were potential thieves. The instant the door opened and the bell over the door ding-a-linged, Mrs. Katz would call out in a raspy voice full of terror, "Who is it? What do you want? I'm a poor old woman!" As a result, Mrs. Katz's business did not flourish as it had when Mr. Katz, with his warm smile and welcoming nature, was alive. Customers who might otherwise have patronized Katz's these days instead went out of their way to Cohen's, preferring "the cranky Cohens" to "the *kvetchy* Mrs. Katz."

Like everyone else, Joel was intimidated by Mrs. Katz and seldom patronized her store. However, today he was coming not to buy but to apply for a job, prepared to offer Mrs. Katz a great opportunity: he would assist her behind the counter and revive her failing business with his energy, personality, talent, and passion and restore her good name and former success. So he approached Katz's with atypical courage and determination.

A hidden cat squealed as he entered the shop. Mrs. Katz, also hidden, squealed: "Who is it? What do you want? I'm a poor old woman!"

"It's only me, Mrs. Katz —Joel Sachs," he called cheerfully.

Mrs. Katz appeared from her hiding place, the back room of the store. She was very short, barely five feet tall, and very stout. She wore a long white apron that was spattered with stains of a variety of syrups and ice cream flavors. Her hair was white, shaped into a bun on the top of her head, and covered in a red hair net. She wore no makeup except for too much rouge on her cheeks. When she walked, she rocked from side to side like a ship in a storm.

"Whaddaya want here?" she asked gruffly. "You're Cohen's customer."

"I wanna talk to you about something, Mrs. Katz," Joel answered coolly.

"You came to *talk*, not to *buy*?"

"I'm looking for a job."

Mrs. Katz was wide-eyed. "A *job*?"

"Yes."

"That's a good one," said Mrs. Katz, taking a wet rag and wiping off the counter.

"I think I can help your business," said Joel.

"What 'business'?" asked Mrs. Katz. "I don't have no 'business'!"

"That's what I mean," said Joel with authority. "I have a lot of great ideas about how to bring in the customers."

Before Mrs. Katz had a chance to throw him out, Joel started outlining his business plans. He explained to her that his great passion was chocolate, and that his passion would transmit itself across the counter and eventually by word of mouth throughout the East Bronx, where his chocolate creations would entice new customers. He spoke with exceptional conviction. He gestured with his hands for emphasis and raised his voice for nuance. He was inspired. He was eloquent.

When he finished his spiel, Mrs. Katz was smiling benignly.

In a tone that for her was unusually gentle, she told Joel that she appreciated his offer. She said she could certainly use help. "Ever since my husband died, I'm alone in the store fourteen hours a day, six days a week." (She closed Saturdays for the Sabbath.) "It's too much for me. I'm all aches and pains."

"I can imagine," said Joel with understanding and compassion. "I mean, at your age and all."

"But"—Mrs. Katz's smile turned sour and her voice dark— "what can I do? I don't have no money to pay help."

Without a moment's hesitation, Joel countered, "Oh, you don't have to pay me a lot. I'll settle for two dollars a week and some stuff."

"Stuff? Whaddaya mean, stuff?"

"You know, candy," said Joel, "and ice cream and stuff like that."

Mrs. Katz grew wary. "How much stuff?"

"As much as I need."

Mrs. Katz was silent and reflective for a moment. Then she spoke. "I can see you eat a lot."

Joel became defensive. "So what's the big deal? You get the stuff wholesale, don't you?"

"It still *costs*," barked Mrs. Katz.

"But I'm only asking for two dollars a week," said Joel. "Who else could you get for that little?"

Mrs. Katz looked down her nose at him. "You'll really work for just two dollars?"

"Yes," said Joel. "And I'll work very hard. I'll bring in a lot of new customers, you'll see."

"You won't steal from the cash register?"

He was about to say, "I don't steal," but he caught himself and said instead, "Pinkies to God." He kissed his pinkies and held them heavenward.

Mrs. Katz chewed on her bottom lip. She scratched her forehead. She walked back and forth behind the counter, rocking as always from side to side, weighing Joel's offer. Finally, she stopped pacing, looked at Joel, and said simply, "So okay."

Joel would start work tomorrow. His hours would be Monday through Friday after school (about 3:30) until he had to be home for dinner (about 6:30) and all day Sunday, from nine in the morning to nine at night. For as long as it took him to learn the business according to "The Katz Way," as she called it, she would work with him and teach him. At first, he would do nothing but menial chores—stocking the candy and cigarettes, filling syrup containers, opening fresh cartons of ice cream, washing glasses and spoons, wiping off the counter, and sweeping out the store. All the while, he would observe Mrs. Katz filling orders and making change. Eventually, when she decided he was ready, she would give him the opportunity to work the counter, taking orders, filling them, and ringing up the sales. When she was confident that he had mastered the Katz Way then—"and only then"—would she trust him to be in the store alone. At that point, she would have three hours daily to herself during the week, and all day Sunday: a true gift.

Joel asked Mrs. Katz what she meant by the Katz Way. Mrs. Katz smiled mysteriously and said, "You'll watch me, you'll find out."

Joel's heart fluttered with excitement. He realized that when he told Mrs. Katz earlier, in an effort to get the job, that his dream was to work in a candy store, he was telling the absolute truth. And now his dream was about to be realized.

At dinner that night, Joel announced his new employment.

The first response was from Fanny, who exclaimed, "Katz?

She's a total bitch!"

"I can handle her," said Joel.

"A candy store?" said Gloria, excited. "Can I come and visit you sometimes?"

"Sure," said Joel. "I'll even make you a sundae or a malted or something."

"Any flavor I want?"

"Any flavor," said Joel.

"Strawberry?"

"Sure."

"Yum," said Gloria.

"How much is she paying you?" asked Lou.

Joel said proudly that he'd be earning two dollars a week.

Lou said, "Two dollars? For how many hours?"

"I'll be working after school and all day Sunday."

"Are you nuts?" asked Lou.

"Don't, Lou," said Rose. "Be proud of him that he got himself a job."

"*Proud*? Two dollars a week I should be proud?"

"Katz is a bitch," Fanny repeated.

"It's slave labor!" said Lou.

Joel said, "I don't care about the money. It's a candy store, and that's my dream."

"Sure," said Fanny. "You'll probably eat up the profits when Katz isn't looking."

"Mind your own business, Fanny," said Rose. "You earn more, but you don't go to school like Joel. Who told you to quit?"

"And you still live here, but do you help with the rent?" Lou asked.

"Whaddaya want from me?" Fanny asked. "I give you and Mommy five dollars a week. How much more do you expect?"

"Do we always have to fight about money when we're having supper?" moaned Gloria.

Rose said, "Gloria's right. No more fighting. Joel got a job, so let's celebrate and eat supper without fighting."

"I lost my appetite," grumbled Lou. "I can't believe I have a son who's so dumb that he takes a job that pays two dollars a week!" He got up from the table and went into the living room to watch TV.

The next day, from the moment he woke up until school was out, Joel was so happy and light-hearted that he forgot to miss the chocolate bars he didn't have. Instead, he thought only of all the chocolate he would have later when he got to Katz's.

He arrived there at 3:25 full of energy, and greeted his boss with a perky, "How are you today, Mrs. Katz?"

Handing Joel a long white apron, more soiled than her own, she answered, "How am I? I'm a nervous wreck, that's how I am. I never had anybody working for me before."

"You won't be sorry," Joel assured her. "You'll see."

"Don't talk so much and get busy. The floor is filthy."

During the three hours Joel worked his first day, only seven customers came into the store. Four of them, Mrs. Katz informed him, were new faces, and they bought only cigarettes. The fifth, the shoemaker from next door, who, Mrs. Katz said, was "her nicest and most loyal customer," bought a candy bar. Then a gentle old man with a cane came in and ordered an egg cream. Joel watched Mrs. Katz make it with more foam than seltzer and not enough chocolate syrup or milk. When the old man left, Mrs. Katz asked Joel if he noticed how she skimped on the old man.

Joel nodded and asked, "How come?"

"The Katz Way," she said with a wink.

"That's the Katz Way?" asked Joel, dismayed. "You skimp?"

Before Mrs. Katz could respond, a grouchy old woman with a hunchback entered and ordered a vanilla malted. Mrs. Katz put two big scoops of ice cream into a malted can, about a quarter of a cup of vanilla syrup, a spoonful of malt, and enough milk almost to fill the can. The old woman drank it all down in less than five minutes. Mrs. Katz asked her how she'd enjoyed it.

"It was all right," said the woman. She paid for it and left.

Mrs. Katz asked Joel, "You saw how I overdid it?"

Joel nodded.

"The Katz Way," said Mrs. Katz.

"I don't get it," said Joel. "You skimp on a nice old man and you call it the Katz Way, then you overdo it with an old lady who doesn't even smile, and call it the Katz Way."

"Right," said Mrs. Katz. "The old man, his son drinks, so I punish him. The old lady, her hunchback breaks my heart, so I give her extra."

Joel didn't say what he thought of the Katz Way, but he privately made a decision to disregard it.

When there were no customers and he had carried out all his chores including filling the syrup pumps, Joel asked Mrs. Katz if he could try something.

"Try what?" asked Mrs. Katz, biting her lower lip.

"To make something."

"It's too soon."

"For *myself*, Mrs. Katz. A hot fudge sundae."

"Before dinner?" said Mrs. Katz. "You'll ruin your appetite."

"No, I won't," said Joel. "I have a big appetite."

"That's what worries me," said Mrs. Katz. "How many scoops?"

"Just two," said Joel.

"Just?"

"With an egg cream on the side."

"An egg cream, too?"

"That way I'll learn to make *two* things."

"It's too much."

"Oh, come on, I earned it, Mrs. Katz. I worked hard today."

Mrs. Katz, too tired to argue, relented. "So okay—a hot fudge sundae and an egg cream. But only one scoop of ice cream."

"I'm working three hours for you, and all I'm asking for is a two-scoop sundae, an egg cream, and eight Nestlé's bars."

"*Eight Nestlé's?* Are you crazy?"

"That's how many I need for tomorrow," explained Joel.

"For *what?*"

"For snacks in school."

Mrs. Katz would have turned him down in no uncertain terms if she didn't recognize that he was a bargain at twice the price. She watched, unhappy but resolved, as Joel smushed two enormous scoops of chocolate ice cream into a sundae dish, smothered them with gobs of hot fudge sauce and topped them with a huge mound of whipped scream squirted from a pressurized can. He finished the sundae off by planting two maraschino cherries at the peak of the mound.

"God in heaven!" said Mrs. Katz.

Smiling broadly, Joel carried the sundae around to the customer side of the counter, sat down on a stool, and, moaning with pleasure the whole time, wolfed it down with tremendous speed. Then he returned behind the counter, washed out his dish, and prepared an egg cream that was more than half syrup and milk. Mrs. Katz, aghast, smacked her cheek as she watched him drink it as if it were a glass of water.

"You'll put me out of business."

As Joel was leaving the store, he helped himself to eight Nestlé's bars.

"Who can eat so much candy?" Mrs. Katz called after him.

"Me," Joel called back. "See you tomorrow, Mrs. Katz." And he was gone.

Gloria was waiting for him when he arrived home. "How was your first day at the candy store?" she asked.

"Fantastic!" said Joel. "I made a great hot fudge sundae." He gave her one of the Nestlé's bars. "Here, sweetie. A special present for you."

"Oh, Joel, thank you!" exclaimed Gloria as she ran to a private place in the apartment to wolf it down.

That night, Joel found that his sexuality was totally reactivated, and he slept like a baby.

Over the next few days, Mrs. Katz saw Joel develop into a first-rate counterman. She was amazed at how quickly he learned the business—especially when it came to making anything that had chocolate as the essential ingredient. By the fourth day, Mrs. Katz was so pleased with his accomplishment and so convinced that he was ready to go it alone, that from then on she gave over full responsibility to him during the three hours he was there on weekdays and the twelve on Sunday.

Business was usually slow, but Joel had ample opportunity to prepare almost every specialty available in a candy store. Mrs. Katz would often surprise him by arriving on his watch without notice in order to check up on him, but all she ever saw was that Joel was a hard and enthusiastic worker, he was good with the customers, he always made the right change, and he could be trusted. True, he did not employ the Katz Way: he was generous to everyone, and he helped himself to a lot of the profits in every form of chocolate. But he never asked for anything more than his two-dollar salary each Sunday at closing time, and the chocolate treats he needed.

Soon, business was showing definite signs of improvement: the number of customers and purchases increased each day. So Mrs. Katz closed her eyes to Joel's chocolate extravagance. She ignored the gigantic portions of ice cream, candy, and soda which he consumed. And as business improved, so did the old woman. She became calmer, less paranoid, and even more generous, especially to Joel. One Sunday, as Joel was collecting his salary and the next day's worth of Nestlé's bars, she urged him to "take more, darling, take a couple extra bars for tomorrow." Joel left with ten bars, two of which he later presented to Gloria.

Mrs. Katz's voice was not as shrill as it used to be. The panic was all but gone from it. When a customer entered the store now, even when Joel was not there, she attempted to greet the customer as Joel did, with a smile and a simple, warm, "Hello, what can I do for you?" The customers clearly appreciated it. They started returning.

One Sunday night, after Joel finished work and got his two dollars, he stopped at Cohen's on the way home. The Cohens were not happy to see him.

"I hear you're working for Katz," said Mr. Cohen.

"That's right," said Joel, and he handed Mr. Cohen the two dollars. "This is for most of the Nestlé's bars I borrowed."

"Two dollars?" said Mr. Cohen. "How many did you steal?"

"One dollar more will cover it. I'll pay you next week."

He left feeling proud.

One afternoon, Rose surprised Joel by bringing Gloria to the store. Joel introduced them to Mrs. Katz, who happened to be there spying on Joel. She was more gracious than Joel had ever seen her. She told Rose that she had a very nice son. "He's a big help to me."

"I'm sure he is," said Rose. "He's a good boy. Everybody loves him."

To Gloria, Mrs. Katz said, "You're a pretty little girl. Do you like your brother?"

"I love him," said Gloria.

"That's nice," said Mrs. Katz. "Give your mother and sister whatever they want," she told Joel. "On the house."

Rose asked for an egg cream, Gloria a black-and-white ice cream soda. Joel overdid it for both of them. Gloria got three scoops of ice cream, Rose got almost half a glass of chocolate syrup. They both raved about their treats.

Mrs. Katz was all smiles. "That's the Katz Way," she told them. She hugged them as they were leaving.

On his own in the store one Sunday, between customers—there were about fifty that day—Joel worked on the first treat he had conceived in his fantasies before he had been hired by Mrs. Katz: a thick chocolate malted with broken pieces of Nestlé's chocolate at the bottom of the glass. He began with two inches or so of syrup, then added a tablespoon of malt, four scoops of chocolate ice cream, and milk almost to the brim of the can. As he worked, he tried to think of a name for his creation, assuming it would turn out as well as he believed it would. While the concoction was mixing on the malted machine, he decided to call it "Joel's Fabulous Chocolate Frosted Float."

He poured the rich mixture into the glass over the Nestlé's pieces and was about to test it, when he realized this was a special moment he didn't want interrupted. He went to the front door, locked it, and hung a sign in the window: "Back in Five." Then he sat down at the counter to have his first taste. It was beyond his imagination—creamy and chocolatey, the most satisfying drink he had ever tasted. It was more than a drink. It was so thick, he had to eat it with a spoon, and he relished every mouthful. When he reached the bottom, he had some difficulty getting at the Nestlé's pieces, but when he did, it was worth the effort. It was the most original aspect of the creation—his personal touch.

Later, when he was alone in the store, he drew a big sign introducing

Joel's Fabulous Chocolate Frosted Float
Four Fabulous Scoops of Chocolate Ice Cream
Two Fabulous Inches of Chocolate Syrup
One Fabulous Tablespoon of Malt
Malted Can Filled to the Brim with Milk
One Fabulous Nestlé's Chocolate Bar Broken Into Pieces
Only 50 cents

Glued to the sign was a Nestlé's bar. Under it, a smiling face. Joel hung the sign conspicuously over the counter.

Mrs. Katz stopped in shortly before 8 P.M. to check on Joel. "So how did it go?" she asked.

"Great," said Joel. "I had about seventy customers."

"Seventy?" Mrs. Katz was amazed.

"I made fifteen sundaes, thirteen ice cream sodas, twenty malteds, a lotta egg creams, and a lotta cones"

Mrs. Katz, although impressed, was distracted by the new sign over the counter.

"What's that?"

Joel smiled. "Just something I thought up."

Mrs. Katz looked more closely at the sign. Suddenly, she threw back her head, hit herself hard on the forehead, and shrieked, *"Four scoops?"*

"It's a come-on, Mrs. Katz," Joel said.

"Only fifty cents for four scoops?"

"It could bring in a lot of customers."

"And a whole Nestlé's bar?"

"It's a gimmick."

"Gimmick-schmimmick. You'll cost me a fortune!"

Joel pulled himself up tall, took a deep breath, and spoke, not in his usual voice of a boy but in his new voice of a man. "Now look, Mrs. Katz, I'm trying to make a success out of this business. One of my ideas is to invent special concoctions that will get people talking about Katz's—especially kids. Which means I have to give them stuff they never had before. And I have to charge them what I think they can afford. If you start getting cheap on me, then let's forget the whole deal. I'll go save some other candy store."

Mrs. Katz, her chin resting between her grandma breasts, listened carefully to Joel. When he was finished, she stared hard at him and said with a shrug, "Do whatever you want. I give up."

In bed that night, Joel felt amazing. Stronger, more mature. As if something very important was happening to him.

*   *   *

Over the next few weeks, Joel invented several new chocolate creations, each more extravagant than the next, but all for the same fifty cents. For each one, he made a detailed sign. There was:

Sachs's Superb Special Split
Five scoops of chocolate ice cream
A whole banana
Hot fudge
Whipped cream
50 cents

and...

Joel's Nestlé's Nourishment
Three scoops of chocolate ice cream
Four melted bars of Nestlé's milk chocolate
Smothered in whipped cream
Topped with chocolate jimmies
50 cents

and...

Sachs's Dynamic Chocolate Duo
A chocolate ice cream soda
A three-scoop chocolate hot fudge sundae
A pile of whipped cream
Three maraschino cherries
50 cents

After each invention, Joel closed the store temporarily, tested what he had created, and then went into the back room. There, based on the size and strength of his erection and the pleasure of its release, he determined whether or not his newest treat was a worthy expression of his powerful imagination.

Oddly, however, no one ordered any of his inventions for

weeks. Many customers inquired about them but seemed to think they cost too much or sounded too rich and might give them a stomach ache. Mrs. Katz thought Joel and his concoctions were *"meshuga,"* but since no one was ordering them anyway, she let it go. Joel was surprised that customers weren't clamoring for them, but this lack of immediate success was not enough to discourage him. He was certain his creations would catch on soon. In the meantime, he decided, while he waited for success he would develop bigger and better combinations and announce them on bigger and better signs.

One Sunday, alone in the store, Joel was composing a sign for his latest come-on:

Joel Sachs's Most Fantastic Chocolate Feast
A four-scoop hot fudge sundae
A combination of Mounds Bar and M&Ms
Whipped cream
50 cents

A chubby girl about Joel's age entered. He smiled as he always did and said, "Hi, what can I do for you?"

"Oh, I don't know," the girl said, looking around the store as if for an idea. "I'd like something unusual."

Joel's heart leapt as he sensed that this could be the moment he'd been waiting for. With her rolls of flesh covered by a coat that strained to stay buttoned, this girl could be a kindred spirit, a chocolate freak like him, someone who would order one of his sumptuous inventions.

"If you want something unusual, you've come to the right candy store," he said, indicating his signs above the counter.

"I don't live around here," said the girl. "I'm visiting my grandmother. She said you give big portions, so I figured I'd try you out."

"Your grandmother's right," said Joel. "I do give big portions. And"—he pointed to his hand-made signs—"I make a lot of unusual creations."

The girl studied the signs. As she did so, she casually asked Joel how much he weighed.

Joel was thrown. "What?"

"I weigh a hundred sixty-five," she said. "You?"

"I'm not sure," he lied.

"More or less?" asked the girl.

"I'm not sure," he repeated.

"I'm very good at guessing weights. You're probably about a hundred and ninety."

Joel was unnerved, silenced by the girl.

"I think I'll try 'Joel's Fabulous Chocolate Frosted Float'," she said, studying the signs.

"Good choice," said Joel, "if you like chocolate."

"'*Like* it'?" replied the girl. "I go nuts for it."

"Then you won't be disappointed." He got right to work.

The girl leaned over the counter and watched his every move, squealing with joy with each scoop of chocolate ice cream Joel placed in the malted can, and clapping her pudgy hands when he added six squirts of chocolate syrup, two heaping teaspoons of malt, and about a pint of milk.

As Joel attached the can to the malted machine, the girl said, "I better warn you: I get all hot and horny from chocolate malteds."

Joel knew exactly what she meant, of course, but he was surprised to hear it from a girl.

"Me, too," he said.

"Great," she said.

While the mixture was blending, Joel broke a Nestlé's bar into pieces and stacked them at the bottom of the glass.

"Oh, God," shrieked the girl. "Catch me if I faint!"

Her response was so gratifying to Joel that he rewarded her with a second Nestlé's bar in the glass.

"Do you know what you're doing to me?" moaned the girl.

When the shake was ready, Joel took it off the machine, poured it into the glass over the chocolate pieces, added a big dollop of whipped cream, and placed it with a spoon on the counter.

"Here you go," he said.

For a moment, the girl didn't touch it. She just sat staring at it with admiration, licking her lips, and muttering, "Oh, God! Oh, God!" She sniffed it and tasted the top layer of foam and sighed with deep pleasure. Then she took her spoon and dipped into it. After one taste, she exclaimed, "Oh, help, oh, this is too much! Oh, God, you're a genius!" She shoveled spoonful after spoonful into her mouth without pausing for breath, moaning and sighing and gasping with the pleasure of profound delight.

"This is without a doubt the most fantastic thing I ever tasted!"

As Joel watched the girl relishing his concoction with all that energy and passion, a strange and unexpected thing happened to him. He started to feel nauseated. Seeing her wolf down the float, he saw himself as if he was looking into a mirror, and it disgusted him. A human pig. That's what she was. That's what *he* was. In about seven minutes her glass was empty, and she smiled at Joel with Nestlé's-covered teeth that made him squirm and struggle not to vomit. The girl's pleasure in his invention had the opposite effect on him than he had anticipated. The surprise of it made his head spin.

"You wanna make out?" asked the girl.

Joel was startled. "Huh?"

"Look at me: I'm wet from your malted," she said pointing between her legs. "Come on, let's make out."

"I can't," said Joel, his voice quaking. "I'm working."

"You can close for a few minutes. I come very fast when I'm this hot."

"I really can't," said Joel.

"I'll let you do whatever you want to me."

"I don't wanna do anything."

"You can lick chocolate syrup off my boobs."

"No, thanks."

The girl pleaded. "I *have* to make out."

Joel could feel his penis shrinking.

"Please," she begged.

"I can't," said Joel.

"Why?" asked the girl.

"I don't feel so good," said Joel.

"Don't you like girls?"

"Some," said Joel.

"Does that mean you don't like *me*?"

Clearing the girl's empty glass and malted can off the counter and wiping it clean with a damp cloth, he tried to explain to the girl. "It's not about liking you. It's about fooling around. You know what I mean?"

The girl started yelling. "What's wrong with me?"

"Nothing," said Joel, feeling guilty and cruel. "I just don't feel like it."

"I thought you said you get all hot and bothered from chocolate, too," she squealed.

"I used to," said Joel.

"How much do I owe you?" she asked, irate, reaching into

her purse for her wallet.

"Nothing," said Joel. "It's on the house."

"Don't do me any favors," said the girl in her fury. "Here's your damn fifty cents, and you can go to hell!" She got off her stool, turned, and walked to the door. Before she left, she turned back to Joel and gave him the finger. Then she was gone, slamming the door and almost shattering the glass window.

Joel wasn't certain what had just happened except that he'd experienced a sudden powerful change, a clarity unlike any he'd known, as if he might be starting out on a new journey to the rest of his life.

A while later, Mrs. Katz came in to close up the shop for the night. "So? How did it go today?" she asked.

"It was a fabulous day," said Joel. "The most fabulous day of my entire life."

"That's nice," she said.

"I'm quitting, Mrs. Katz."

"What?" she asked, certain she hadn't heard right.

"I'm quitting," Joel repeated.

The old woman asked, "Why? What's wrong? Did I do something bad? Did I say something?"

"No, it's not you. You've been very good to me. It's myself. I have to get away from all this chocolate. I'm giving up chocolate altogether."

Mrs. Katz was incredulous. "You? Joel *Fresser*? You're gonna give up chocolate?"

"Yes," said Joel. "Starting today I'm a different person."

"What if I pay you more? Maybe a dollar more a week?"

Joel replied, "It's not about money, Mrs. Katz. It's about my heart and soul. I'm not a kid anymore. It's time for me to stop the chocolate."

Mrs. Katz leaned her head into her right hand, rocked back and forth, and whined, "What am I gonna do without you, Joel? You're my whole business."

"I'll help you find someone to replace me, don't worry. I'll teach him everything there is to know. I'll train him to be as good as me."

Mrs. Katz bawled.

At bedtime that night, Joel undertook to test his resolve. When his mother offered him his usual nighttime snack of Mallomars and chocolate milk, he declined for the first time ever.

Rose stared at her son in disbelief. "You're sick?"

"No, Ma, I just don't want any more chocolate."

Rose couldn't believe her ears.

Later, in bed, while Fanny snored, Joel realized he had gone without chocolate since early that afternoon, before the chubby girl came into the shop. Yet even after more than six hours of a chocolate fast, he managed to sustain a healthy erection for almost ten minutes and, using his manly right hand, reached another extraordinary orgasm.

Rhonda Spiegel

From the time he stopped working at Katz's candy store in 1953, Joel Sachs was cured of his chocolate addiction. By 1955, when he was sixteen, he had lost about thirty pounds and grown about three inches. He was not exactly slim, but neither was he fat. That year, he was invited to his first Sweet Sixteen party.

Leonore Grossman lived directly across the street from Joel, but he didn't know her well. They went to different schools and hung out in different crowds. Their mothers were better friends than they were. One day, Joel's mother told him that Leonore's mother had informed her that Joel was invited to Leonore's Sweet Sixteen party on Saturday night.

"Why her mother? Why not Leonore?" Joel asked.

"Leonore is shy," his mother's answered.

"I'm shy, too. I won't know anybody there."

Joel didn't want to go because he wasn't experienced at going to parties, except family events—weddings, bar mitzvahs, holiday, and birthday parties. Not that he wasn't social. He had plenty of friends, but all of them were boys. He was a mess in the presence of girls.

His mother said he had to go to Leonore's party. It was time for him to start meeting girls: "For heaven's sake, Joelly, you're sixteen years old, and you've never even been out on a date. You're a terrific dancer, but Fanny is the only girl you've ever

danced with. You're going to Leonore's party, and that's final."
As an afterthought she added, "And I expect you to dance."

Joel's eight-year-old sister, Gloria, defended him: "It's not
fair to force a person to do something he doesn't want to do."

Rose said, "It's fair if you're his mother."

The next day, Joel met his father after work at Ben Gershon's
Clothing Store For Men on Southern Boulevard to get a suit
for the party. Lou worked at Boulevard Men's Clothes, a few
blocks south of Gershon's. Boulevard and Gershon's were
vicious competitors.

"You realize I'm taking you to a different men's store than
Boulevard?"

"Of course, I realize it," said Joel, "and I don't get it."

"How many fathers do you know who would buy their son a
suit retail that they could get at twenty percent off in the store
where they work?"

"You're the only one I know, Dad," said Joel. What he didn't
say was that he thought his father was nuts for not shopping
in the store where he'd worked for the past fifteen years, and
where he could get the same suit for less money. But Joel
always thought his father was a little strange. Like the time
Lou bought him a spiffy Schwinn two-wheeler for his eighth
birthday. He could have had the bike for half the price, but he
had to show off by purchasing all the accessories—a basket, a
bell, a light, a fur cover for the seat—which almost doubled the
price. When he couldn't meet the monthly payments less than
three months later, the store threatened to repossess the bike,
so Lou had to borrow money to pay it off. Or the time he gave
his wife two dozen roses for Valentine's Day and taped a dollar
bill to each stem, which Joel thought was so romantic. But the

next day Lou got a mysterious phone call and asked Rose for the twenty-four dollars back to pay a gambling debt. Weird behavior from Lou wasn't all that surprising to Joel.

The salesman approached them as they entered Lou's competition.

"What can I do for you two gentlemen?" he asked.

"You can help me find my boy the best suit you have," Lou replied, as if he were a man of means. "Price is no object."

"No problem," said the salesman, smiling and studying Joel critically from head to toe. He disappeared for a few minutes and returned with five different suits. Joel liked three of them, but his father didn't like any and wound up picking one off the rack himself: a double-breasted blue gabardine. It was clear from the face the salesman made that he thought it was a mistake. And so did Joel. He hated it.

"I like that gray one better," Joel told his father, referring to one of the suits the salesman was carrying.

"I don't," said Lou. Holding up the blue one he had selected, Lou said, "Try this one on."

"Shouldn't it be *my* choice?" asked Joel.

"Who's paying for it?" Lou snapped. "When you pay for your own suit, the choice will be yours."

"But it's a suit for an old man," Joel protested. "No kid I know wears double-breasted."

"Are you crazy? Who's the expert here—you or me? Double-breasteds are the best suits. The only kind I ever wear."

Which was true, and another example of Lou's weirdness. After all, he worked in a store filled with all kinds of suits, many of them much snazzier than the ones he wore. Joel thought his father had awful taste in clothes.

"That's my point," said Joel. "Double-breasted suits look better on old men than young ones."

Lou was offended. "You're calling me an old man?"

"That's not what I mean," said Joel, and he went to the dressing room to try on the suit.

"You get more material for your dollar in a double-breasted jacket," his father insisted to the salesman. "Isn't that so?"

"I guess so," said the salesman, "but your son's right about one thing: young men usually wear single breasted suits unless they're exceptionally tall and thin."

"Are you gonna tell me you know better than me what my son should wear?"

"No, sir," said the salesman. "You're his father, I'm sure you're right."

"Anyway, Joel is tall," said Lou. "Maybe not so thin, but very tall."

Joel wasn't by any means very tall, except perhaps by contrast to Lou, who was only five feet six inches.

Joel returned from the dressing room in the suit. Lou studied him, turned to the salesman, and said, "Look at that. Perfect. He looks like a man instead of a kid. I'm sick of looking at him in ugly dungarees all the time."

"I like my dungarees," said Joel.

Lou ignored this and said, "This suit fits you like a glove. It doesn't need any alterations except cuffs. Do you know how much money that will save me?" Then he turned to the salesman. "How much are you asking for this? It better be a good price." When the salesman told him the suit was forty dollars plus tax, Lou called him a lot of names, including "crook" and "*gonniff*," which mean the same thing.

When the salesman saw what an iffy sale this was going to be, he started brown-nosing Lou, assuring him that he had excellent taste and that the suit was "genuine gabardine" and worth twice the price.

"I'm not spending forty dollars on a boy's suit," Lou said firmly.

"If I charge you any less," the salesman pleaded, "I'll lose my job."

"Let me talk to the manager," Lou demanded and winked at Joel as if to say, "Watch your father in action."

"What's the problem here?" the manager asked as he approached.

"The problem is the price of this suit," said Lou. "Forty dollars plus tax for a *boy's* suit?"

"It's a *man's* suit," said the manager. "This is the *men's* department."

"Does this kid look like a man to you?" Lou asked, poking Joel in the arm. "Maybe he's a little big for sixteen years old, but look at him closely: you call this a *man*?" He pinched his son's cheek hard. "Baby fat," he grunted. "I'm in the business myself, I know every trick in the book, so just give me a bottom line price and we'll call it a day."

The manager nodded. "How much is it worth to you?" he asked.

"I wouldn't give you more than twenty-five dollars for it tops."

"Make it thirty, and it's a deal," said the manager.

"And no tax," said Lou.

The manager resisted. "It costs *me* tax, too."

"No tax or no sale," said Lou. "And free alterations."

The manager was incredulous. "Free alterations, too?"

"You want the sale or not?"

The manager wanted it.

If Joel didn't like the suit before, watching his father hustle the store manager and seeing the manager almost grovel made him *despise* it, especially after Lou had insisted earlier that price was no object. At the same time, Lou seemed happier than Joel had ever seen him. He kept patting Joel on the back, telling him how handsome he looked, something he'd never done before. When they left the store with the suit, he said to Joel, "What you just saw happen is why they call your father a genius salesman."

"Albert Einstein," muttered Joel.

"Damn right," said Lou, who had no sense of irony. "A forty-dollar suit for twenty-five dollars *and no tax* and *free alterations.*" He laughed. "They were pushovers. No customer of mine could ever talk me into that."

"Is that why you shopped here instead of Boulevard?" Joel asked him. "So you could prove how great you are and make fools of them?"

"I always knew I was a smart salesman," said Lou, "but I wanted to find out if I'm also a smart customer. It turns out I am."

On the way home, they stopped at Woolworth's so Joel could buy a present for Leonore. His father reluctantly left it to Joel to pick it out because, as he said, "I don't know the girl."

"I hardly know her myself," said Joel.

"Well, all I can tell you," said Lou, "is women like perfume. The first present I ever gave your mother was a bottle of *Evening in Paris*, the cheapest perfume on the market, and she loved it."

So Joel chose a bottle of *Evening in Paris* for Leonore.

On Saturday, Joel appeared before his family in the blue gabardine suit with a white dress shirt from his bar mitzvah three years before and his father's red tie, which had a coffee stain on it. His mother squealed with surprise and delight. Her eyes filled with tears as she looked him over.

"My Joelly is growing up so fast."

Joel checked himself in the mirror to see what she was carrying on about. What he saw reflected was someone in a ridiculous double-breasted suit. He asked Gloria what she thought.

"I think you look very nice," she said.

Eighteen-year-old Fanny didn't agree. "You always think he looks nice," she said to Gloria, "even though he looks like a *schlep*."

"I look like a *schlep*?" Joel asked.

"Yes," said Fanny, "but you can't help it."

"Don't say another word, Fanny," said Rose.

"Fine," said Fanny. "It's against the law to tell the truth in this family. Anyway, I'm in a rush. I'm supposed to meet this guy from work in twenty minutes." She hurried out.

"He didn't want this suit," Lou said to Rose. "Can you believe it?"

Surprised, Rose said to Joel, "You didn't want this gorgeous suit?"

Lou said, "He's lucky I got him what *I* wanted, not what *he* wanted."

"Since your bar mitzvah I never saw you look so handsome," said Rose. "When I look at you, I see a lot of me."

This from a woman who was about five feet two inches, stubby, and wore black muumuus down to the floor everywhere she went to cover her protruding belly and enormous breasts. Fanny referred to her behind her back as "Rosie five-by-five."

"The tie looks good too, huh?" said Lou. "I got that for Chanukah from my boss about five years ago."

"It has a stain on it," said Gloria.

"It came that way," Lou lied.

"I'll get it out," Rose said, and she did—with soap and water and a lot of rubbing.

Minutes later, with a wet tie and a bundle of nerves, carrying a gift-wrapped package of *Evening in Paris*, Joel left the house and crossed the street, his mother watching proudly from the window. He rang Leonore Grossman's bell. Her mother opened the door, a big woman dressed as if it were *her* Sweet Sixteen, in a girlish pink chiffon dress, pink shoes, and a pink bow in her hair. She gave Joel a warm smile.

"Oh, Joel, I'm so glad you came."

"Hello, Mrs. Grossman." He could hear the nervous tremor in his voice, but he couldn't control it. "Thanks for inviting me."

"Leonore will be so happy you're here."

She led Joel by the hand into the living room, where the furniture had been pushed against the walls and pulled him through the roomful of noisy, sweaty dancing teenagers—Joel did not know a single one of them—all dressed in their best clothes. She delivered him to Leonore, who was giggling with a group of her girlfriends.

"Look who's here, Leonore," Mrs. Grossman announced. "It's Joel from across the street."

"Oh, hi, Joel from across the street," Leonore said, and turned back to her girlfriends. The giggling resumed. Joel assumed they were laughing at him, and he crumbled inside.

Suddenly, lights were lowered, the record player blasted Kay Starr singing "Wheel of Fortune," and couples danced close. Mrs. Grossman abandoned Joel to elbow her way onto the dance floor and separate those whose bodies were touching.

"Enough, Marty. Give Eva some breathing room." Then, "Back up, Eddie. If you get any closer, Irene'll wind up pregnant."

As Rose constantly reminded him, Joel was a good dancer thanks to Fanny. She was otherwise rotten to him, but she had spent a lot of time teaching him how to dance. Of course, she taught him only so she'd have someone to partner with at family functions, but she did teach him every step she knew. The problem that night was that he didn't have the experience or nerve to ask any girl to dance, so he was probably going to have to disobey his mother and be a wallflower. He was miserable. He went over to the food and drink table and helped himself to a Ritz cracker piled high with tuna fish, which he nibbled as he watched the others dance and neck.

It was then that he first saw Rhonda Spiegel. She was standing alone on the other side of the room, swaying to the music. She was without a doubt the most beautiful girl Joel had ever seen—except in the movies. She had jet-black hair, bobbed in tight curls all over her head, blue-violet eyes, soft pink skin, and bright, wet red lips. She reminded him of Jennifer Jones, one of his favorite movie stars.

As he watched her, he caught her eye and she smiled at him, so he smiled back. Moments later, waving her arms and swaying to the beat of the music, she sashayed across the floor and up to him. He began to have difficulty breathing.

"Dance?" she asked without the least self-consciousness.

His heart was pumping at a frightening pace. "Um…sure," he answered.

"Do you know how?" she asked.

"Yes," he said. "My older sister taught me."

"Let's see if your older sister was a good teacher."

They danced. Rhonda wasn't very good. She moved her hips too much—something Fanny directed him never to do—and she tended to lead rather than be led, which made it hard for Joel to move her around the floor. But he didn't care. He felt privileged to be holding this exquisite girl in his arms. Nothing else mattered.

After a few minutes of two-stepping to Nat King Cole's "Unforgettable," she said, "Your sister's a good teacher."

It was at that moment that Joel fell in love with Rhonda.

He drew her a little closer. She smelled like a garden. She was even more beautiful than Jennifer Jones. She looked like Elizabeth Taylor, which added to her stature in his eyes. After all, Jennifer Jones was beautiful, but Elizabeth Taylor was the most beautiful movie star in the world and much sexier than Jennifer Jones.

Rhonda's body was soft but firm. Joel's hand felt comfortable against her back, like it belonged there. She seemed comfortable in his arms, too. After a few minutes of dancing, she leaned in closer and put her cheek against his, creating powerful sensations inside him.

"Your sister should open a dancing school," she said.

"I like dancing with you more than my sister," he said.

"Well, I should hope so," she said, and they laughed.

Moments later, Leonore's mother was moving them apart with her strong hands.

"You'll suffocate her," she said to Joel.

"Oh, I don't mind," said Rhonda.

"*I* mind," said Mrs. Grossman. "I'm from an older generation."

"Sorry," said Joel, embarrassed.

"Why doesn't anybody dance with Leonore?" Mrs. Grossman asked him. "She's the Sweet-Sixteen girl, after all. Don't you think she's pretty?"

"Sure," he said. "She's very nice looking."

"You should dance with her. She's a wonderful dancer. Why do you think I invited you?"

"Well, I'm dancing with someone right now, Mrs. Grossman," said Joel. "Maybe I'll dance with Leonore a little later."

Mrs. Grossman frowned. "If I see the two of you dancing that close again, you're out of here." And she was gone.

Rhonda grunted and muttered, "Mrs. Bossy."

"True," said Joel, but he didn't attempt to move in closer. The last thing he wanted now was to be thrown out.

"Somebody else can dance with Leonore," said Rhonda.

"I don't even know her very well," said Joel. "I live across the street from her, but we never say anything to each other except maybe hello."

"She's in my homeroom class at Columbus," said Rhonda. "But we're not really friends. I was surprised she invited me. I mean, I'm not in her crowd, and she's not in mine."

"I was invited because our mothers are friends," said Joel. "I almost didn't come."

"Well, I'm glad you did," said Rhonda.

"So am I." He was close to panting.

Someone changed the record, and the music switched to rumba: Dinah Shore singing "A Rainy Night in Rio." The rumba was Joel's specialty, and Rhonda was impressed. She said that dancing with Joel made her feel like a better dancer than she was. He didn't say anything in response to that. He didn't want to seem conceited, and he certainly didn't want to hurt her feelings by saying anything negative about her dancing, even though she kept tripping over her own feet and stepping on his with her pointy high heels. She never apologized. She just giggled. And after a while, instead of trying to avoid it, Joel began to look forward to each pounce on his foot. It felt like a love tap.

Rhonda lived about eight blocks away, so when it was time to go, Joel offered to walk her home.

"I expected you to," she said.

As they walked, Joel tried to figure out how he could take her hand and hold it without making an ass of himself. But before he could come up with a strategy, Rhonda took his hand in hers, surprising and delighting him.

They talked about their schools. She went to Columbus, an ordinary high school in her Pelham Parkway neighborhood. He lived nearby in the adjacent Allerton Avenue neighborhood, but he went to the Bronx High School of Science, a special school for boys that was more challenging than most public schools and a long subway ride away. Rhonda didn't much like school, which she admitted with some giggles. She couldn't wait to be through with high school so she could get married and have a family.

"I'm dying to know what it feels like to be pregnant," she said.

Joel loved school and took it very seriously. He intended to go to college and become a teacher. But he didn't tell Rhonda that. He didn't want to suggest any difference in attitude toward school for fear it might alienate her. So he implied that, like her, he was unserious about school and schoolwork. She seemed to appreciate that, although she said she didn't understand how someone who didn't like school could pass the test for Bronx Science.

"The boys I know who go to Bronx Science are all so..." she searched for the appropriate word..."*intellectual*. And they get such good grades."

"I know what you mean," said Joel, "but I'm nothing like that. I mean, I get okay grades, but I'm not an *intellectual*."

All the way home, she mocked her classmates or made snide remarks about them. One girl had buckteeth. Another had frizzy hair. Yet another had terrible skin. Rhonda was clearly a snob, mainly about looks.

"There was this boy last year when I was a sophomore," she told Joel, "and I had a real crush on him, but no matter what I did, I couldn't get him interested in me. It made me very upset. I mean, didn't he even think I was *pretty*?"

"I think you're beautiful," said Joel.

"That's what I mean," said Rhonda. "Most boys do. Why didn't *he*?"

Joel hardly heard what she was saying. As she talked, his thoughts had more to do with kissing her than listening to her angry judgments. Should he dare try to kiss her at the door when he dropped her off? Would she be offended? Or would she expect it? Would she think there was something wrong with him if he didn't try? If he did try and she let him kiss her, would she also let him stick his tongue in her mouth? It was a tremendous, overwhelming dilemma. His friends always talked about getting to first base and then moving on to second and third. He didn't actually know what took place on any of those bases, but he could imagine. He decided first base must be the kissing base (did that include kissing with the tongue?), and he struggled with the notion of reaching it tonight. He *had* to, he told himself. I'm *sixteen*. I'm *ready*.

When they got to Rhonda's apartment, they stood in the hallway at the front door, staring at each other in silence for a few moments. Joel started perspiring. Rhonda smiled. Joel took her smile to mean she was inviting him to first base. He leaned in. She backed away.

"It's too soon," she told him. "It's only our first date."

"Oh," he said, disappointed.

"I don't want you to think I'm fast," she said.

"I won't," he said. "I swear I won't." He kissed his pinkies to heaven.

Rhonda giggled.

Suddenly, the door opened, and Rhonda's mother appeared, startling Joel and ending the possibility of his getting to any base tonight.

Mrs. Spiegel was, like Leonore Grossman's mother, a big woman. She had a somewhat prettier face than Mrs. Grossman, but otherwise the two mothers seemed interchangeable.

"I was starting to worry," said Mrs. Spiegel.

"Why?" asked Rhonda.

"It's after eleven," said her mother.

"That's not so late."

"How was the party?"

"Fun," said Rhonda. "Joel's a great dancer."

"So introduce us already," said her mother.

"This is Joel."

"Hello, Joel," said Mrs. Spiegel. "I used to be a good dancer, too, when I was your age—long before you were even a sperm in your father's eye."

"Nice to meet you," said Joel, surprised to hear a mother use the word *sperm*.

"Come inside, don't stand in the hall," said Mrs. Spiegel. She left them at the door, expecting them to follow, and walked back into the apartment.

Joel thought about leaning in again to kiss Rhonda but stopped when she said, "If you'd like to go on another date with me, my number is in the phone book. Under Annette Spiegel. That's my mother."

Joel said he would definitely like to take her out again and he'd definitely call her. "Can I come inside?" he asked.

"I'm too tired," she said. She entered the apartment and closed the door.

"Goodnight," he said to the door.

As he walked home, Joel was filled with self-loathing. Why didn't she let me kiss her? What's a kiss? It's no big deal. Unless I have bad breath. He breathed on his hand and smelled it. It's not bad, he decided. Then he yelled silently at himself, Why'd you take no for an answer, schmuck? You could've reached first base with those hot red lips waiting for your tongue, and now you've missed the chance. But then he thought, at least I'll have a second chance. I'll take her out next week and make sure I get on base then—I won't take no for an answer.

He also thought about the fact that she didn't like school and probably wasn't a good student. That might have put him off another girl, but he sensed that Rhonda had a bright mind even without liking school. Even if she isn't so bright, he told himself, who am I to judge her? Sure, I go to Bronx Science, but so what? There are plenty of dummies at Bronx Science. And plenty of bores. It occurred to him that even if she thought he was intelligent, maybe she found him boring. That's why she didn't kiss me. I'm so boring.

He was beginning to drown in self-hatred when he stopped himself, switched gears, and let in some sunshine. Think about that face, he told himself. Think about the fact that a beautiful girl liked me enough to hold my hand. True, she didn't let me kiss her, but maybe she would have if her nosy mother hadn't interrupted. And she said she'd go out with me again, didn't she?

By the time he reached home, he was a changed Joel. He entered the apartment and saw his parents sitting on the living-room sofa, watching TV in their bedclothes. His mother, as usual, wore a muumuu, this one yellow with purple and red flowers that she wore only to bed. His father was in his boxer shorts and undershirt. Joel blurted out, "I met a girl from Pelham Parkway, I danced with her, I took her home, she said I'm a good dancer, I'm going to take her out next Saturday again, thanks for making me to go to the party, Ma."

All this happened without Rose or Lou having asked a question or even greeted him. Which was unusual. Normally, the minute he walked in the door, his mother assaulted him with one question after another: "How was school?" "How did softball practice go?" "How was the sandwich I made you?" "How was the movie?" "Are you sure your friend Danny is a nice person? To me he looks like a hoodlum." Joel normally hated her questions and always tried to avoid answering, but tonight he *wanted* them. He was a different person from the boy who had left the house earlier. He felt grown-up, and he wanted his parents to know it.

Instead, what he got from his mother was, "Not now, Joel, we're watching Jimmy Stewart." And from his father, "Keep it down! This is one of my favorite movies!"

He was hurt and disappointed. He started for his room but stopped short and asked himself what kind of parents they were. How could they be more interested in Jimmy Stewart than in their own son? He returned to the living room and announced, "Her name is Rhonda Spiegel, and she looks like Elizabeth Taylor."

His mother looked at him as if he were a lunatic and said, "That's nice, Joelly. Go to bed." And his father yelled, "Quiet, both of you! I'm trying to hear the TV!"

Joel turned and stormed to his room, locked his door, and was about to throw off his clothes and get into bed when a snore from Fanny reminded him that this wasn't his room alone. Fanny and he still shared this bedroom. So he went into the bathroom for some privacy, stripped naked, lay down on the bath mat on the floor, and masturbated three times in a row to fantasy images of Rhonda dressed, semi-dressed, and undressed. Then he stood up, wrapped himself in a towel, got into bed naked, and fell asleep.

Breakfast was normally Joel's favorite meal, but the next morning he had no appetite. He tried to drink his orange juice but spilled most of it on himself. He refused his mother's French toast, which she made out of challah and cooked in about a quarter of a pound of butter, so it was dense and rich. Joel was usually wild for it.

"Why aren't you eating?" Rose wanted to know. "You love my French toast."

"I'm not hungry."

"What is with you?" she asked. "You were goofy last night and you're goofy today. What happened last night?"

Which infuriated him. Last night, when he tried to tell her about Rhonda, she wasn't interested. In his anger, he made a decision to punish her: what happened between Rhonda and him was hereafter personal and secret, especially secret from his mother and father. So now, of course, Rose was curious.

"I don't feel like talking," said Joel. "I'm going for a walk. I don't know when I'll be back."

"You want me to go with you, Joel?" asked Gloria.

"No, sweet thing," he said. "I need to be by myself." And out he went.

His heart was racing, his legs twitching. He was a wreck—enraged, anxious, horny. He thought about going over to his best friend Izzy's apartment and telling him about Rhonda and how he'd fallen in love last night, but he decided against it when he realized that Izzy would probably start teasing him, and that would make him even angrier and, lead to a fight. Instead, Joel wandered aimlessly around the neighborhood, thinking about Rhonda, which got him hard. He walked for blocks and blocks with an erection poking at his pants.

He passed Cohen's Candy Store on the corner of his block. After a moment's deliberation, he walked in, went straight to the phone booth, dropped a nickel in, called information, got the number for Annette Spiegel on Lydig Avenue, committed it to memory forever: ME3-4285. He retrieved his nickel, redeposited it, dialed the number, and tried to catch his breath while Rhonda's phone rang.

When Rhonda answered, Joel's heart stopped. When she said she had been hoping he would call, he felt dizzy with delight. When he asked her if she would go out with him next Saturday night ("We could go to a Broadway show"), she said, "I'd love to. I love show songs, but I've never seen a Broadway show." He thanked her profusely, which he later thought must have confused her. In the normal world, *she* should have thanked *him* for the invitation. But who was in the normal world? Not him.

When he got back home, Gloria was watching TV in the living room. "You feel better, Joel?"

"Yes, honey," he told her. "You don't have to worry about me."

"You wanna watch TV with me?"

"No, thanks," he said and went into his room to think some more about Rhonda and Saturday night. Fanny wasn't home, so he had the room to himself and was able to enjoy himself to images of Rhonda Spiegel performing unspeakable acts.

On Tuesday, after school, he went by subway downtown and bought two balcony seats to a revival of the musical *Oklahoma!* at the City Center. The tickets cost two dollars and eighty cents each, which he paid for with money he'd saved from birthday gifts and Chanukah *gelt*. He felt the same sense of maturity he had felt when he gave up chocolate. It was as if by meeting Rhonda and asking her out on a date and paying for theater tickets with his own money, his transformation into manhood had clearly taken hold.

That week as he waited for Saturday, Joel was unnaturally slow-witted and dull, and his teachers noticed. Mr. Schreiber, his math teacher, was shocked when he sent Joel to the blackboard to solve an easy equation in advanced algebra, and Joel was unable to figure out where to begin. Mrs. Harley in ancient history asked him a question about the Roman Empire, and he didn't know the answer. He wished he could announce to her, to the class, to the entire world that he hadn't been able to concentrate on his homework the night before because he'd fallen in love with the most beautiful girl in the Bronx and she had taken over his brain. But he didn't say a word. Given that he was famous for being one of the top students at Bronx Science, his sluggishness in class was a surprise to everyone. He simply wasn't himself. All he could think about was Rhonda, taking her to see *Oklahoma!* Saturday night, and possibly getting to first base and—if there really was such a thing as a miracle— maybe even to second base.

He spent Saturday going crazy trying to figure out what to wear that night. He couldn't wear the suit his father had bought him for Leonore Grossman's Sweet Sixteen party for two reasons: first, Rhonda had just seen him in it, and second, he hated it. But the rest of his wardrobe was limited to dungarees and flannel shirts or tee shirts, and he wanted to look great for Rhonda on their first official date, especially because they were going to a Broadway play. He had nothing appropriate except the suit, so in the end, he wore just the pants and the only shirt he owned that would go with the pants, the same white bar mitzvah shirt he'd worn to Leonore's party. He could do without a tie, and because it was early spring he decided he could also do without the suit jacket. The shirt was clearly much too small on him—the cuffs settled well above his wrists. He rolled up the sleeves and although he thought he still looked ridiculous, he didn't know what to do about it.

When his mother saw him without a jacket or sweater, that's all she saw. She gasped in horror, assuring him he'd wind up in the hospital with pneumonia, and insisted he wear something warmer or he couldn't go out. He argued passionately that he couldn't wear the exact same outfit two weeks in a row, but Rose was unwavering. "There's nothing wrong with wearing the same thing," Rose said. "The girl won't even notice."

"But I hate this jacket," Joel pleaded.

At this, Lou turned red with rage. "If I hear you say one more time anything bad about that suit, it goes one-two-three to Jewish Philanthropies as a donation."

"Why can't Joel wear what he wants to wear? It's his body," said his one defender, Gloria.

"Butt out of this," said Rose, which silenced her.

Joel wound up wearing the very same outfit he wore last Saturday when he first met Rhonda, minus the tie. Neither of his parents complimented him this time, but Gloria told him once again that he looked "very, very nice." Joel was deeply unhappy. However, it turned out his mother was right about one thing: it was an unusually cold April night, and without the jacket he would have frozen.

The first thing Rhonda said after she opened the door was, "Isn't that the same suit you wore to Leonore's party?" An image flashed through his mind of his parents begging for mercy as he machine-gunned them. He was so humiliated by Rhonda's question that he felt compelled to justify himself.

"My mother made me wear it. She wouldn't let me go out without a jacket. And this is the best jacket I have for going to the theater."

"I think he looks very nice," said Mrs. Spiegel as she appeared from somewhere in the apartment. Joel thanked her, and she said with a warm smile, "You must be a very nice boy if you do what your mother tells you."

Lest Rhonda regard him as under his mother's thumb, Joel replied, "Well, I don't *always* do what she tells me."

Rhonda asked him what show they were going to see. When he told her *Oklahoma!* she squealed like a five-year-old and clapped her hands.

"Did you hear that, Mommy? *Oklahoma!* My favorite!" To Joel she said, "I have the album. I know every song by heart."

"That's great," he said. "We better get going. It starts at 8:30."

Rhonda went for her coat, leaving Joel with her mother, who smiled at him and said wistfully, "I saw *Oklahoma!* with Rhonda's father, may he rest in peace, when it first played on Broadway. He loved the theater. If he was still alive, believe me, he would've taken Rhonda to see it by now. But I'm glad she's seeing it with a nice person."

Joel thanked her, hiding his surprise at learning that Rhonda's father was dead.

"What time do you think you'll be back?" Mrs. Spiegel asked.

"Well," said Joel, "the show will probably be over about 11 or 11:15."

"So late?" she asked, surprised.

"Musicals are usually about two hours plus the intermission," he said.

She nodded. "Of course. It's been such a long time since I went to a Broadway show. My husband died ten years ago already, and I forgot things like that."

Rhonda appeared. Joel helped her on with her coat, which made her giggle.

Her mother said, "You're going out with a *gentleman*, Rhonda." And to Joel she said, "Please take good care of my only child. The world is dangerous. Watch out for bad people."

He promised he would, and they left.

On the way to the subway, Joel told Rhonda how incredible she looked—she was wearing a sexy dark green dress and a fake fur coat that also seemed sexy to him—and how fabulous she smelled.

"It's *Evening in Paris*," she told him.

After she repeated to him several times how excited she was about seeing *Oklahoma!* there was a lull in the conversation. Joel said quietly, "I didn't know about your father. I'm really sorry. That must be hard for your mother and you."

"I was only six when he died, so I hardly remember him," she said. "If you hardly knew someone, it's hard to miss them much."

Her honesty surprised him and drove him more deeply in love with her.

All the way to the City Center, on the subway and on the street, they talked about death. She said she was terrified of it. Joel told her he wasn't the least bit afraid of it. "When you die," he said, "you don't know it. If you don't know it, what's to be afraid of?"

"The unknown," she said. "That's what scares me. Sometimes, I pretend to myself that I died, and I try to imagine what it feels like. But I can't, and that frightens me because usually I have a fantastic imagination. So if I can't imagine something, it must be really scary."

"In my opinion, death is just another part of life," said Joel.

"How can death be a part of life?" Rhonda asked. "Death means you're dead. Life means you're alive."

Joel was going to defend his platitude with some pretentious profundities, but he didn't get the chance because as they reached the City Center, the crowd going into the theater was so pushy and noisy that they gave up trying to have a serious conversation. Instead, they directed their energies to making their way inside without losing each other.

Joel surprised himself by being a good leader. He managed to get them inside, up two flights of stairs, and into their seats in the last row of the theater in the second balcony.

"Wow," said Rhonda, "I've never been up so high before— except once on a Ferris wheel."

She may not have intended to embarrass Joel, but that's what she accomplished. In self-defense he lied, even though he hated lying: "These were the only seats left."

"Oh, it's okay," said Rhonda. "I'm just happy to be here."

She smiled such a radiant smile that Joel had the impulse— but not the nerve—to grab her and give her a juicy kiss right then and there.

As the audience filled the seats and the orchestra tuned up, Rhonda couldn't seem to sit still. She started bouncing slightly in her seat as if she had to go to the bathroom.

They read the playbill together and discussed the actors, not one of whom they'd ever heard of. Rhonda knew from her record album all the actors' names from the original Broadway production, and she informed Joel of every one: Alfred Drake played Curly, Joan Roberts played Laurie, Celeste Holm played Ado Annie, and on and on through the entire original cast. Except for Celeste Holm, none of those names meant any more to him than the names of tonight's cast. When they came to the song titles as they were listed in the Playbill, Rhonda hid her eyes and said, "Let me see if I can remember them in order," and she proceeded to name each musical number from the overture to the finale in perfect sequence. Joel applauded her, and she giggled with pride.

"Why doesn't it start?" she asked.

He checked his watch. It was after 8:30. "Any minute," he assured her.

"Are you as excited as me?" she asked.

He said he was, and he *was*, but not about *Oklahoma!* His excitement was about being so close to Rhonda in these narrow theater seats that her arm occasionally grazed his. And sitting this close, he was mesmerized by her intoxicating *Evening in Paris* scent.

The lights began to lower.

"Oh, my God, it's starting!"

When the theater was dark, a spotlight discovered the orchestra conductor entering from the wings. The audience applauded him. Rhonda applauded so hard that people seated nearby turned to stare at her in amazement. The asbestos curtain rose, and on the red velvet stage curtain was printed in big gold letters, "O-K-L-A-H-O-M-A!"

More applause from the audience.

Rhonda crowed. "I can't believe I'm really sitting here!" It thrilled Joel to know he was responsible for her delight.

The conductor gave the downbeat, and the overture began. The first melody was "People Will Say We're in Love." Rhonda started singing along: "Don't throw bouquets at me...Don't please my folks too much..." She sang in a squeaky voice often a little off the note, but she articulated every lyric precisely.

"...Don't laugh at my jokes too much...People will say we're in love..."

A woman seated in front of them turned in her seat and told Rhonda, "Please, leave the singing to the actors, dear."

It was too dark to tell whether or not this hurt Rhonda's feelings, but she obeyed the woman and stopped.

As for the show itself, it was easy to sense that Rhonda concentrated all her energy on the stage—the performers, their costumes, the dancing, the music—and absorbed and adored every minute of it. She applauded after each musical number and even shouted "Yea!" a couple of times. When the ingénue finished her "Out of My Dreams" song and ballet, Rhonda was sniffling.

"Oh, God!" she said, "Can you imagine what it must feel like to sing and dance like that with everybody's eyes on you and everyone thinking you're beautiful and loving you and then applauding you?"

Joel was too focused on the question of whether or not to put his arm around Rhonda's shoulders to pay much attention to the show. His fantasies had to do with the gorgeous girl sitting next to him, not with the actress on stage. By intermission, he had managed to get as far as holding her hand through "Many a New Day." When that song ended, however, she pulled her hand away in order to applaud. And when the applause was over and Joel tried to take her hand again, she whispered to him, "Your hand is too sweaty." Possibly the worst thing she could have said, it left him feeling totally diminished through the rest of the first act and made it impossible for him to try putting his arm around her. His arm was probably sweaty too. If perspiration was to be the measure, reaching first base that night did not seem likely.

When the lights came up for the intermission, Rhonda was so flooded with the emotion the show was producing in her that she didn't want to leave her seat. Joel asked her if she'd mind his leaving her alone for a few minutes because he had to use the bathroom. That made her giggle, which added to his embarrassment. He had to walk down three long flights of stairs to get to the men's room and then wait on a long line to get in. By the time he started upstairs again, bells were ringing, signaling the start of the second act. But as he passed the orchestra section, he noticed a candy counter, and he decided to stop and surprise Rhonda with a bag of M&M's. When the counterman told him it was 50 cents, Joel thought for a moment about putting it back. 50 cents for M&M's seemed outrageous when the same size bag cost ten cents at any candy store in the Bronx. After all Linda, his family's latest cleaning woman, got paid only two dollars for spending all day cleaning their apartment. But then he remembered why he wanted the M&M's, paid the 50 cents, and rushed up the stairs to Rhonda. It was dark by the time he sat down, and the second act overture was in progress. Rhonda was bouncing in her seat again. Joel showed her the bag of M&M's.

"Oh, thank God," she said. "I'm starved." She stopped bouncing.

During the second act, they watched the stage and shared the candies. The bag was in her lap, and Joel made a point of reaching in for an M&M at the very moment Rhonda's hand went into the bag so that their fingers touched. By about the fifth touch, he managed to take hold of her hand. During "The Farmer and the Cowman Should Be Friends," he found the courage to move his free hand along the back of her chair and let it rest gently on her shoulder. She didn't object, so he left it there for the rest of the show, believing now that first base was definitely within reach.

When the final curtain came down, Rhonda was on her feet along with much of the audience, cheering the cast and shouting "Bravo!" The moment they left the theater, she started singing the entire score of the show. Just as Joel hadn't cared that she wasn't a good dancer, so he ignored the fact that she was a pretty bad singer. He loved listening to her. In fact, he loved everything she did. It was magical. She could do no wrong.

On the subway back to Pelham Parkway, Rhonda started singing almost at the top of her voice: "There's a bright golden haze on the meadow...There's a bright golden haze on the meadow...The corn is as high as an elephant's eye..."

An old man sitting nearby, shouted, "Hey, knock it off, girlie! You're croakin' like a frog!"

Rhonda stopped singing immediately. She was so hurt that her eyes welled with tears and she even stopped speaking. She didn't say a single word for the rest of the subway ride and entire walk to her apartment. Joel kept trying to engage her in conversation, asking her about movies she might have seen, books she might have read, and friends they might have in common, but she ignored everything he asked.

"I think you're making too much of what an old man said," he told her. She didn't respond. So he added, "You shouldn't take him seriously, he was probably drunk." She disregarded that, too. "As far as I'm concerned," he concluded, "a person should be allowed to sing whenever and wherever she wants." But nothing he said appeased her.

As they walked to her apartment house, Joel commented occasionally on the weather, which was almost wintry. He even tried talking about *Oklahoma!*, reminding her of moments he knew she'd loved—as when Laurie did her ballet or Ado Annie sang "I Can't Say No"—but he could not break her silence.

When they reached her door, she took her key out, unlocked it, and was about to enter her apartment without a word, but Joel stopped her by saying, "Um…I hope you had a nice time."

"I had a very nice time until you know when," she replied. "That horrible old man managed to ruin the whole night for me."

"'The whole night?'" he asked, surprised. "Even *Oklahoma!*"?

"No, I loved *Oklahoma!*" she said.

"I hope we can go out again," he said tentatively.

"Call me," she said, "and we'll discuss it."

He moved towards her for a kiss, but at that moment, her mother's large frame appeared and she asked, "So how was it?"

"The show was fabulous, but the rest was awful," Rhonda answered. Surprised, Mrs. Spiegel asked, "What 'rest'?"

"A man on the subway insulted her singing," Joel explained.

Rhonda turned to her mother and added, "He said I croaked like a frog." In tears again, she ran past her mother into the apartment and disappeared.

Her mother smiled at Joel. "She's very sensitive about her voice, but she'll be okay." Mrs. Spiegel closed the door. Joel's evening with Rhonda was over and kiss-less once again.

He left her building disappointed and thought to himself, "Well, at least I got to put my arm around her. Maybe next time I'll get further." As an afterthought he recalled that she had soft shoulders, and immediately he got hard.

As it turned out, Joel didn't get to kiss Rhonda until their sixth date. Up till then, she found a way to avoid a goodnight kiss every time he brought her home from the movies, where they spent almost every date after the first. Twice she turned away saying to him, "You better not get too close. I think I'm getting a cold." Both times he told her the same thing: "I wouldn't mind catching a cold from you." She laughed and waved him off. Once she turned her head away just at the moment of mouth-to-mouth contact, claiming to have heard a distracting noise. And once, before he had a chance to attempt to kiss her, she headed straight into her apartment, said good night, and closed the door in his face. Each of those times, as he walked home, he told himself that he shouldn't tolerate such treatment. He would give her an ultimatum: put up or shut up. If she didn't put up he would stop seeing her. After all, their dates were costing him two movie tickets and popcorn and Cokes every two weeks, and he was beginning to feel exploited. But the thought of never seeing her again seemed far worse than being used by her and kept him coming back for more.

By the sixth date, however, as they approached her door after the movies, he surprised himself by finding the courage to say, "I hope tonight you'll invite me in."

She seemed thrown by that. She probably would have found a way out of it if at that same moment her mother hadn't opened the door and said, "Why don't you invite Joel in, Rhonda? I'll make some hot chocolate for the two of you."

Rhonda hesitated.

"I love hot chocolate," said Joel. "My mother makes it for me every morning in the winter."

"So come on in," said Mrs. Spiegel. "We'll see who makes better hot chocolate, Rhonda's mother or yours."

Rhonda did not seem happy as she followed her mother inside. But Joel, of course, was ecstatic as he tailed Rhonda and closed the door behind him.

"I'll go make the hot chocolate," said Mrs. Spiegel.

When she was gone, Rhonda and Joel looked at each other.

Again Joel surprised himself. "How about showing me your room?"

Rhonda seemed baffled. "My room?"

"I bet it's great."

Rhonda shrugged. "It's a room." But she took his hand and led him in.

What Joel saw was a lot of pink: a pink dresser, a pink desk, a pink chair, a mirror framed in pink, pink walls, pink curtains, pink linens, and photos of Rhonda everywhere, looking her most beautiful, all framed in pink. He studied everything with fascination. When his gaze reached the bed, he got hard and looked at Rhonda, who was standing there expectantly.

"So?" she asked.

"How come we never kiss?"

Rhonda frowned. "I thought you were going to say something about my room."

"It's nice," said Joel, "but how come we never kiss?"

"We hold hands, don't we? I let you put your arm around me, don't I?"

"Yes, but I'm ready for kissing."

"I have a thing about kissing," she said.

"What kind of thing?"

"Germs."

"I don't have any germs."

"Everybody has germs."

"So how come other people kiss?"

"Look, Joel, I don't like kissing, and that's all there is to it."

Joel was as shocked as Rhonda by what happened next. Without another word, ignoring her resistance, he moved up to her, put his hands on her shoulders, drew her close, and went to kiss her. His lips were an inch away from hers when she turned her head, and all he got was her cheek.

"Okay?" she asked. "Are you satisfied?"

"No," he said. "I want lips."

"I can't," she whined.

He refused to accept it. He grabbed her and this time succeeded in kissing her on the mouth before she had a chance to turn her face away. She tried to break his hold on her, but he wouldn't let her. He kept his lips pressed against hers until she surrendered and actually began to kiss him back. It turned out to be pretty hot. He considered sticking his tongue in her mouth, but that thought passed quickly. A tongue kiss might seriously upset a person who worried about germs. So he satisfied both of them with just a mouth-on-mouth kiss.

When it was over, he asked her if she was planning to wipe off his germs. She smiled coyly and said she was not. He tried to kiss her again, but she became rigid.

"Once is all you're allowed," she said. "You better go."

"But your mother's making hot chocolate," Joel protested.

"I'll tell her you had to get home."

"Why do you want me to go?"

There was a long pause before she answered. "If you must know, I have women's troubles." She blushed.

"Oh," he said, "I know about that. My older sister gets bad cramps when she gets her women's troubles."

"Me, too," said Rhonda. I have terrible cramps."

"Okay," he said. "Next Saturday night?"

"Call me," she said, "and we'll discuss it."

She led him to the front door. Before he left, he pecked her on the mouth, catching her off guard. She giggled.

"I hope your women's troubles aren't contagious," he said.

She laughed and closed the door after him.

From then on, one kiss per date became the ritual. The kiss got longer and juicier, but she never permitted more than one. Even one Saturday night, when they went together to a birthday party for a friend of Rhonda's, although all the other couples were kissing and necking, Rhonda reminded Joel when he tried for a kiss that one kiss was all he'd be getting that night, so if he chose to kiss her then, that would be it until their next date. He held her very close, he breathed in her ear, he nuzzled her neck, but he resisted kissing her in order to save it for later when they were alone in her bedroom. Of course, since he couldn't even get to first base more than once a date, it was clear he would never go beyond.

And so it went all through junior year. They dated about twice a month—Joel couldn't afford her more often than that, especially after the ninth or tenth date, when they started going for pizza or ice cream after the movies. In the theater, he'd put his arm around her and hold her hand as long as his hand stayed dry. They'd usually share M&M's or popcorn and a Coke—from two different straws, at her germ-phobic insistence. When he took her home, she'd invite him in, they'd watch TV together until her mom said goodnight and went to bed, then they'd go into her bedroom, sit on her bed and kiss—once. A couple of times they lay down facing each other on the bed and kissed in that position, which was hotter. But after the one kiss, she'd always escort him to the door.

One time Joel asked Rhonda on the phone who she went out with when it wasn't with him.

"Who said I go out with anybody?" she teased.

"Do you?" he asked.

"None of your business," she giggled.

He persisted. "Come on, Rhonda, please tell me."

"It's none of your business," she repeated, this time without the giggle.

"I'm just curious to know what you do on Saturday nights when you don't go out with me."

"Curiosity killed the cat."

All that year, with just handholding, an arm around her shoulder, and one kiss every other Saturday night, he never lost his desire for her. In fact, the more she withheld, the more he hungered for her. Her looks and her body, which became more extraordinary the longer he knew her, compelled him most, but in fact everything about her appealed to him, even her version of germphobia, which allowed only one kiss per date.

In late May of that year, sitting in her bedroom, Joel asked Rhonda to his junior prom. It was the big event of the school year at Bronx Science because it was preparation for the senior prom the following year. The junior prom was held in the school gym, whereas the senior prom took place in a hotel ballroom. Gowns and tuxedoes were required at the senior prom, but juniors could wear their "Sunday best." The senior prom ended at 1 A.M., the junior prom by 11 P.M. But it was as important to go to the junior prom because those juniors who didn't go were considered "losers." So when Rhonda turned him down, Joel was not only shocked and his pride injured, but he was also worried about his reputation at school.

"You mean you really don't want to go to the prom with me?" he asked, as if she had turned down the greatest opportunity of her life.

"It's not that I *don't want* to go, it's that I *can't*."

"Why not?"

"I can't tell you."

"Why not?"

"I just can't."

Joel told her what the consequences would be for him if he didn't go, how he would be perceived at school.

"Then take someone else," she said coldly.

"I don't want *someone else*," he said. "I want *you*."

This irritated her and she snapped, "Okay! You want to know why I can't go with you? It's because I'm going to my own prom. At Columbus."

Joel was shaken.

She continued. "Is it unreasonable that I want to go to my own junior prom?"

"No," he said, "but who are you going with?"

"Really, Joel, you ask too many questions that are none of your business."

"So that means you're going with another guy. And that means you've probably been dating him while you've been dating me. And that *is* my business. And I'm not sure I want to see you anymore."

Of course, at the moment, it was an empty threat, and they

both knew it. Even when he hated her, as he did now, he was still madly in love with her. He knew as well as she that nothing he said could change her mind and that nothing she did would make any difference. His jealousy only fed the flame of his love.

"It's up to you if you stop seeing me," she said and told him it was time for him to go home.

"Can I have my kiss?"

"No."

"How come?"

"Just go."

For the next few days, Joel was so depressed he couldn't function. His entire academic future was at risk because of the poor performance he was giving in school thanks to Rhonda. Gloria was so sensitive to his moods that she knew how unhappy he was, and she did everything she could to cheer him up. She bought him candy and cookies and ice cream with money that she'd saved from her meager allowance and assured him it was all right to stuff himself with junk if that would lift his spirits. She told him funny stories about her teacher and the kids in her class. He felt so guilty for causing her worry that he decided to phone Rhonda and ask her if she'd perhaps changed her mind and, if not, didn't she want to reconsider? She answered no to both possibilities. Joel hung up more depressed and miserable than ever. That night he wrote her a letter.

> *Dear Rhonda,*
> *I've never been so hurt by anyone in my entire life. We've been going out for almost a year, I've taken you to the theater and a lot of movies, and I've spent a lot of my money on you.*

And you think it's okay to turn me down for my prom and not even think of inviting me to yours. I don't know who else you're dating, but he must be a lot better than me. A lot better looking. A lot better built. A lot smarter. A lot richer. If that's what he's like, I don't blame you for liking him more than me. Under the circumstances, I think we should call it a day. I'm sure you'll be happy to know you won't be hearing from me again.

Sincerely,
Joel Sachs

Despite his conviction when he dropped the letter into the mailbox, he regretted it immediately. He missed Rhonda desperately. Not just seeing her, but hearing her voice on the phone, making plans for each Saturday night, holding her hand, touching her shoulder, sniffing the *Evening in Paris,* and claiming his one kiss. And he was more than slightly distressed about not being able to go to his prom. He barely studied for final exams because he couldn't think clearly and feared that he would wind up for the first time in his high school career with several grades lower than A. He found it difficult to eat, and when he did eat, digestion was a problem. But he never considered calling Rhonda again and trying to convince her to resume their relationship. He was too hurt and too angry. She made him feel like a boy again. She'd robbed him of his manhood.

Her response to his letter the following week shut the door on any hope of reconciliation.

My dear Mr. Sachs,
I received your high and mighty letter, and all I can say is that I can't help it if I'm more attracted to someone else than I am to you. You may be a nice person and you may be

*intellectual enough to go to the Bronx School of Science, but
the other boy I'm dating suits me better than you do even if
he isn't as intellectual as you. And yes, he is better looking,
and he does dress better, and I do enjoy kissing him more
than you, and I'm sorry if this hurts your feelings, but I
always try be honest about my emotions.*

    Goodbye forever,
    Rhonda Spiegel

A few weeks later, Joel was leaving for school one morning
when he saw Leonore Grossman coming out of her house
across the street. He smiled and waved to her. She smiled and
waved back.

"Going to school?" he called.

"Yes," she said.

"Me, too." He waved again and started walking on, but then
he stopped suddenly and called across to her, "Hey, Leonore,
would you like to go to my junior prom with me?"

"What?" she asked, surprised. "You want to take *me* to your
prom?"

"Yes," said Joel. "It's this Saturday night. I could pick you
up at seven."

"Okay" was all she said.

Which was how he got to go to his junior prom after all.

Rose was ecstatic when he told her he was taking Leonore
Grossman.

"Oh, that's wonderful, Joelly. I'm crazy about her mother."

Gloria was less enthusiastic. "Leonore's not pretty enough
for you."

Fanny was, as usual, mean. "You're right, Gloria. Leonore
Grossman is funny-looking with those *braces*."

Rose said, "The braces will fix her teeth, and she'll be adorable."

Joel wasn't all that enthusiastic about Leonore replacing Rhonda with her perfect white teeth, but he was relieved to have a date. He wore the same blue gabardine double-breasted suit he'd worn to Leonore's Sweet Sixteen party and then again to the theater with Rhonda. He was taller and thinner these days, so the trousers were a little baggy and a little short, the jacket sleeves were also short, and the waist was loose. But there was no time to have the suit altered. He also wore the same bar mitzvah shirt, which was now more than four sizes too small.

"You look gorgeous," said his mother.

His father reminded him, "If it weren't for me, you would never have such a handsome suit for your prom."

Gloria said, "You look very, very nice, Joel."

Fanny didn't comment. She didn't have to. Her sour expression said it all.

Leonore looked lovely in the same dress she had worn to her Sweet Sixteen, and she complimented Joel on the way he looked, too. "I love that suit," she said with genuine enthusiasm. Although she wasn't nearly the beauty Rhonda was, she had, except for her braces, a pleasant-enough face and a soft and gentle personality, different from Rhonda in a very important way: Joel felt *comfortable* with Leonore—less desperate, unpressured. They had a fun time at the prom. They danced and ate and laughed a lot with Joel's friends, and when they said goodnight at her door, Leonore not only let him kiss her, but she opened her mouth for his tongue and took his hand and placed it on her breast. After which they said good night and parted.

Joel crossed the street to his building feeling victorious. He was happy to have gone to his prom with Leonore Grossman, happier than if he'd gone with Rhonda Spiegel. Leonore wasn't vain. Leonore appreciated him. Leonore was, in fact, sexier than Rhonda. That became clear to Joel when he got into bed, realized that his member was throbbing more powerfully than ever, grabbed it, and massaged it with tremendous pleasure.

In the dark, a voice—Fanny's: "Oh, somebody had a good time tonight."

A Squirrel and a Couple of Nuts

After a day of teaching, Joel Sachs was in the waiting room of his dentist's office, reading *The Great Gatsby*, anticipating the two hours or more he would have to wait for Dr. Klein, the family dentist whose patient he'd been since he was a child. He didn't like Dr. Klein, who had not changed his equipment and techniques since Joel first started coming to him almost twenty years ago. Klein didn't believe in using Novocaine except for pulling teeth, and being a Leninist, he talked non-stop about the horrors of capitalism. But despite his overbearing personality and old-fashioned and often painful dentistry, he had kept Joel's teeth in such perfect condition that Joel had stayed with him.

There were, as usual, several other patients ahead of Joel today because Klein's scheduling methods were as eccentric as everything else about him. If another patient called and asked to see him at a particular day and time, even if six other patients had been scheduled for that time, the dentist instructed his receptionist to agree to a seventh appointment, especially if the request was from a long-standing and loyal patient. As a result, Joel was never the only one scheduled at a given time. But he put up with it and came prepared, usually with a novel, to wait for as long as necessary.

On this particular day, about a week after Joel's twenty-fifth birthday, Emily Goldblatt entered the waiting room, and went up to the receptionist, who nodded and told her to have a seat, Dr. Klein would be with her eventually. Emily sat down, picked up *Cosmopolitan* and settled in for the long wait.

Joel recognized her immediately, and he was shocked. He was also upset at being thrown into the past, battered by unpleasant memories of how she had behaved toward him seven years earlier, when they were both counselors at Camp Keeowah. She had destroyed his trust in women, the way Rhonda Spiegel had when he was sixteen and in love for the first time. Like Rhonda, Emily was beautiful, as beautiful sitting in the dentist's office now as she had been when he first met her. Her blond hair was shorter, her breasts fuller, but nothing else seemed to have changed. As he watched her cross her legs and skim the magazine, he had the urge to shout, "Hello, bitch, remember me?" Instead, he only stared at her.

Emily felt his eyes on her and looked up. Joel did not acknowledge her. She smiled her exquisite smile and mouthed, "Joel?" He nodded but remained silent and expressionless. That didn't stop Emily from getting up, crossing the room, and sitting down next to him.

"What a surprise!" she said.

"Yes," he said coldly.

"It's been such a long time," she said.

"Yes," he repeated.

"You look the same," she said.

"You too," he said.

"I think you're even better looking," she said.

Joel shrugged.

"I guess Dr. Klein's your dentist, too," she said.

"Since I was about six years old," he said.

"I was eight when I started coming here," she said. "Don't you think he's weird?"

"Totally," said Joel.

Emily laughed. "His hero is Trotsky."

"Lenin," corrected Joel.

"But he's a good dentist."

"Yes," said Joel.

"So I'm willing to put up with his blather."

"Same here."

"I'm used to it," said Emily. "My father's a leftist, too."

"Oh."

"I just wish Klein didn't keep me waiting so long," said Emily. "Sometimes I spend the whole afternoon here."

"Me too," said Joel. "I come prepared." He pointed to the novel he was reading.

"I love *The Great Gatsby*," said Emily.

"I teach it," said Joel.

"Oh, I'm a teacher too," said Emily. "Of course, my students aren't ready for *The Great Gatsby*. I teach first grade." She laughed. "I'm really happy to see you again."

Joel was silent.

"I guess you don't feel the same way about seeing me," she said.

Joel said nothing.

"You're still angry about what happened between us at camp, huh? I guess your feelings are still hurt."

Joel shrugged.

"Seven years is a long time to hold a grudge, isn't it?"

"I'm not sure what I feel," said Joel.

"I wish I could erase what happened," said Emily, with what seemed like sincerity. "I mean, we were just kids. It isn't as if I didn't like you. I thought you were a wonderful person."

"You just liked Howie Horowitz better," said Joel.

"You have to admit, Howie was really cute," said Emily with

a giggle.

"And what was I? Chopped liver?"

"You were cute, too," said Emily. "The point is, we're different people now. I assume we've both matured a little. I think it's time for you to get over your resentment."

"I can't help what I feel," said Joel. "The minute I saw you walk in, I felt a sting just like the one I felt when I asked you to spend your day off with me and you turned me down because you had a crush on the head counselor."

"Well, Howie and I broke up as soon as camp was over. He went on to Dartmouth, and I went to Hunter. And that was that."

"Good," said Joel. "I'm glad to hear it." He realized that he was behaving like a fifteen-year-old, but he couldn't help it. He was still distrustful of women—of this woman in particular. But, as she said herself, she was no longer the frivolous teenager of Camp Keeowah days. She was a professional woman, a teacher like him, and she seemed so nice, so appealing, so sexy. He decided to change his attitude.

"Are you married?" asked Emily.

"No. Are you?"

"No."

"Are you going with anyone?" asked Joel.

"No."

"I'm surprised."

"Why?"

"Because you're so beautiful."

"Excuse me while I blush."

"Oh, come off it. You know you're beautiful."

Emily laughed. "Some of my first graders think I'm a witch."

Joel began to relax, and for the next half-hour, he and Emily talked about their lives, which for the most part meant talking about their work. Joel told Emily about the literature courses he was teaching at Tiffany Prep, a prestigious secondary school for privileged kids on the Upper East Side, and about the kids he taught there, most of them spoiled brats but exceptionally smart. Emily, in turn, talked about her first-grade pupils, "who are all so bright and so adorable. I just love them."

Joel told Emily about one of his students who kept referring to Ibsen as Isben. "No matter how many times I correct him, he inverts the second and third letters of the name." Emily reacted with a musical laugh that touched Joel's heart the way it had the first day of camp, when they met at counselor orientation.

She, in turn, talked about Janie, a girl in her class who had imaginary arguments with her mother at least once a week at lunchtime. "She opens her lunch box, and she finds an egg salad sandwich. 'Mommy,' she says, 'why do you give me egg salad? You know I hate it.' She then impersonates Mommy. 'Egg salad is very healthy, Janie.' 'I don't want to be healthy,' says Janie, 'I want to be happy.'"

The story delighted Joel, and he laughed.

One of his students, he told Emily, refused to use punctuation of any kind. "He maintained that it interferes with his *style*. I told him, 'It's impossible to understand your essays or appreciate your 'style' without punctuation.' He said, 'Sorry, Mr. Sachs, but that's the way I write.' So I told him, 'Well, *I'm* sorry, Mr. Farrell, but I won't read anything you write unless you punctuate it properly.'"

"Did it work?" Emily asked.

"He quit the class and told the headmaster I'm a rotten teacher."

Again, they laughed.

"One of my kids always forgets to zip up his fly," said Emily, "and he comes to school with his pants open. So I remind him to zip up. Whenever he goes to the bathroom, he comes back unzipped. Once I asked him why. He said. 'My father told me to be proud of what I have and show it off.'"

"His *father* told him that?"

"That's what he said."

"Do you suppose his father walks around unzipped too?"

"I'll let you know when I meet him," said Emily.

More laughter.

About herself, Emily revealed that she loved to dance and sing, read and go to movies and theater, and she loved to cook. Joel told her he loved all the same activities except for cooking. "Theater's been my passion all my life. I don't cook," he said, "but I love to eat."

"It sounds to me like we'd be quite compatible," said Emily.

At that moment, the receptionist called, "Mr. Sachs, Dr. Klein will see you now."

Joel was startled. He'd been so focused on this reunion with Emily that he'd forgotten where he was. He said goodbye to Emily and extended his hand to shake hers. She took his hand and with her magical smile told him how happy she was that they'd run into each other this way.

"I'll probably still be sitting here when you're through," she said.

"I hope so," said Joel.

In fact, when Joel came out of the dentist's office and into the waiting room again, Emily was still there. Joel was holding his cheek. Emily asked him if he was in pain."

"I begged for Novocaine," Joel slurred, "but Dr. *Lenin* refused to give me any. "'You know why capitalists can't take a little pain?' he asked me. 'Because you're all spoiled.' And I couldn't answer him back because the damn drill was in my mouth."

Emily couldn't help smiling, more at Joel's charm than his irritation.

He was about to leave when she said, "By the way, Joel, I'm listed in the Bronx phone book. In Riverdale. I mean, if you ever feel like calling me or anything."

Joel smiled and nodded as well as he was able with his drilled tooth throbbing. Then he left, and Emily continued waiting.

For the rest of that day, there was hardly a moment when Emily wasn't on Joel's mind. He wondered whether or not she had genuinely changed, or if her charm and humor was simply a mask for the Emily of the past. By evening, he decided to give her the benefit of the doubt, called information for her number, and dialed it.

"What took you so long?" asked Emily.

Joel laughed. "I didn't want you to think I was the aggressive type."

"I go for the aggressive type," she said. "How's your mouth?"

"The swelling's gone. How's yours?"

"All I had was a cleaning, which the dental hygienist did. I didn't have to put up with Klein."

"Boy, are you lucky," said Joel.

"I'm glad you called," said Emily, "because my aunt Grace, my father's sister, has offered me the use of her vacation house in Putnam Valley. It's about an hour and a half north of the city, off the Taconic. A really charming house with a lot of land around it."

"Sounds nice," said Joel, wondering what this had to do with him.

"Do you like the country?" Emily asked.

"Sure," said Joel. "My family used to go to the Catskills when

I was a kid, before my father gambled all his money away."

"Oh, your father was a gambler?"

"He still is."

"My father doesn't believe in gambling. He says it's an activity for rich Republicans."

Joel laughed. "Well, my father *is* a Republican—even though he's broke most of the time."

"Anyway, here comes the commercial: my aunt hardly ever uses the house since my uncle died, especially at this time of year when it's starting to get cold. Since Monday's Veteran's Day and there's no school, she asked me if I'd like to use it over the long weekend. I've been thinking of going tomorrow and coming home Monday, except that I'm afraid to be there alone. It's very quiet at night, and very dark."

"Are you inviting me to go with you?" asked Joel.

"Yes," said Emily.

Joel was silent.

"If you'd rather not," she said, "it's okay. I mean, I realize it's short notice."

"I'm just thinking," said Joel.

"Oh," said Emily.

"It's a nice offer, no doubt about it."

"Do you have other plans?"

"No."

"So what then?"

Joel was silent.

"Are you still making your mind up about me?"

Joel didn't reply.

"Well, take some time to think about it," said Emily. "If you decide you want to go, call me back."

She was about to hang up when Joel said, "How would we get there?"

"I have a car," said Emily. "A 1962 Dodge. It's nothing to look at, but it runs like a dream. I take very good care of it."

Again, silence.

"Are you still there?" asked Emily.

"How many bedrooms does the house have?" asked Joel.

The question surprised Emily. "Bedrooms?...Just one."

"So you mean we'd share a bed?"

Emily was even more surprised. "Well, there's a sofa in the living room. You could sleep there if you like."

Silence.

"Are you telling me you don't want to sleep with me?" asked Emily.

"No," said Joel. "I'm just surprised, that's all."

"I'm not a virgin. Are you?"

"No. Of course not."

"So what's the big deal?"

He remembered Rhonda Spiegel, and the memory made him suspicious. Uncertain. His mind was a blur.

With obvious frustration, Emily asked, "So do you want to meet me here at my apartment after school tomorrow? I'm in Riverdale, which is much closer to the Taconic than you are in Manhattan."

"Okay," said Joel without much enthusiasm.

"I don't want to pressure you," said Emily. Immediately she changed her mind. "Yes, I do," she said. "I want to prove to you that I'm a good person and I won't repeat my seventeen-year-old behavior."

"How do I get to your apartment?" Joel asked.

Emily gave him her address and directions to get there by an express bus that made a stop just a couple of blocks from where Joel lived. He wrote down every word. His hand was shaking. He was nervous about sharing a bed and making love to someone he wasn't sure he trusted.

"I can't wait to see you again," said Emily, who wasn't the least bit apprehensive.

Which unsettled Joel all the more. "Goodbye," he said.

"I'm really excited," said Emily.

They hung up.

On Friday afternoon, after his heaviest day of classes—two in the nineteenth-century English novel, one in modern American fiction, one in twentieth-century plays, and a grammar class—Joel left school. He took the bus to his apartment, showered, and packed for the weekend, uncertain of what to bring. He left Manhattan at 6:30 on an express bus to Riverdale. It stopped right in front of Emily's apartment house, where she was leaning against her 1962 Dodge parked at the curb. Joel got off the bus and carried his suitcase to the car. He'd been anxious all the way to Riverdale, and he was more anxious now as he approached her.

She smiled her beautiful smile, showing her perfect teeth, and said, "You made it."

"Yes," said Joel, his voice flat.

As if she could read his mind, she told him, "You won't be sorry" and proceeded to open the trunk of the old Dodge. Joel placed his bag next to hers in the trunk. She started the engine, and while the car warmed up, she leaned over and kissed him quickly on the mouth. Then they drove off.

Joel was thrown by the kiss, but he said nothing.

"I hope you like affectionate women," she said.

Once they were on the Taconic Parkway, moving at a reasonable clip, Emily asked, "Do you think if things had worked out differently, and I hadn't rejected you at camp in favor of

Howie, you and I would be in my car like this on our way to a weekend in the country together?"

"I have no idea," said Joel.

"I don't think we would," said Emily. "I don't think I was ready for you."

"What do you mean?" asked Joel.

"You're the kind of guy a girl falls in love with in a serious way and winds up marrying. You're not just a toy. I was looking for toys back then."

"You mean you're looking for a husband now?"

"I think about it," said Emily. "Does that scare you?"

"A little."

"Don't you want to get married?"

"Not yet. One of my great dreams has always been to be a father. So I guess when I'm ready to have that dream come true, I'll be ready to get married."

"Well, believe it or not, one of my great dreams has always been to be a mother. Since I was a little girl. And *I* know I'm ready for it to happen. So I guess I'm ready for marriage."

"Maybe it's better if we don't discuss marriage and children now," said Joel. "I was hoping we were heading for a weekend of fun, not for anything heavy and serious."

"Have no fear," said Emily. "I still like to play, which is my only intention this weekend."

"That's a relief."

Emily laughed and squeezed his thigh affectionately.

The trip along the Taconic was smooth and light-hearted. Joel and Emily talked more about their work and how much they loved teaching. For much of the ride, they listened to the radio and sang along. They both loved popular music and had pleasant voices. They sang with Ricky Nelson:

I'm a travelin' man

I've made a lot of stops all over the world
And in every part I own the heart
Of at least one lovely girl.

And with Connie Francis:
Where the boys are, someone waits for me,
A smilin' face, a warm embrace, two arms to hold me tenderly.
Where the boys are, my true love will be.
He's walkin' down some street in town and I know he's lookin'
there for me.

Singing relaxed Joel, and he began to forget that he was ambivalent about spending the weekend with Emily. At one point he asked her to pull off at a rest stop so he could use the men's room. When he returned, he asked her if she had to go.

"Yes," she said, "but I never use public restrooms."

"How come?"

"I can't stand the smell."

"That's funny," said Joel. "I love the smell."

Emily was thrown. "Are you serious?"

"Could you fall in love with a man who loved the smell of other people's pee?" he asked.

"Don't make me laugh," she said. "I'll wet my pants."

This made Joel laugh, which made Emily laugh harder, which made Joel laugh even harder.

"Please!" Emily begged, holding her legs together tightly.

They both tried to stifle their laughter, but it wasn't easy. Each time one stopped, the other started.

"Oh, no!" said Emily. "I think I leaked."

"Ooooh," said Joel, "can I smell it?" He started to lower his head towards her crotch.

Emily screamed with laughter. "Don't you dare!"

By the time they reached Emily's aunt's house in Putnam Valley, Joel had moved as close as possible to Emily, so that they were sitting hip-to-hip. Only her left hand was on the steering wheel. Her right hand was between his legs, rubbing his left thigh, not quite touching his genitals. They were no longer laughing. They were panting.

It was dark when Emily pulled up to the house as close as possible to the front door. Both she and Joel burst out of the car and dashed to the door of the house. After fumbling in her purse, she found the key and unlocked the door. Once inside, without a word, Emily took Joel's hand and pulled him into a bedroom. They tore off their clothes. She jumped on the bed and lay on her back as he topped her.

"Don't you want to pee first?" asked Joel.

"I don't have to anymore," she answered.

The sex was passionate and powerful. They kissed and licked and sucked and fucked as if they were virgins. Then, just at they both approached orgasm, Emily screamed in terror and pushed Joel off her. In one small section of the thick molding that ran around the room near the ceiling, she had noticed a patch of gray that looked almost like a ball of dust. But as the bedsprings squeaked, the gray patch unfurled and became a squirrel, which started running along the molding.

"What's wrong?" Joel asked. "Why'd you stop?"

Pointing to the squirrel, Emily shrieked, "Look!" She jumped off the bed and ran from the room, pulling the door shut behind her.

Joel saw the squirrel, shouted, "Fuck!" jumped off the bed, and followed Emily out the door. He discovered her, fully nude, standing near the exit door of the house, trembling.

"Did you get him?" she asked Joel, who was also naked.

"Get him?" Joel asked, as if she were insane. "Me?"

"I'm terrified of rodents," said Emily.

"So am I," said Joel.

"But you're a man," said Emily. "Men are supposed to be brave about such things."

"Not *Jewish* men," said Joel.

"Oh, God," said Emily.

Frightened as he was, this was the moment he'd been waiting for. Under the stress of this incident, he expected Emily to show her true colors, turn on him, and reject him for being less than her image of a man. Howie Horowitz, although he was also Jewish, would probably grab some kind of blunt instrument, run back into the bedroom, and bash in the squirrel's head until it was dead. This was hardly something Joel could do. He couldn't kill an animal unless it was a life-or-death situation.

"I'm really sorry, Emily," he said, "but I'm not going back into that room."

"Well, neither am I," she replied.

"You're still trembling."

"I was about to come."

"So was I."

"*Coitus interruptus,*" she said.

"*Squirrelus interruptus,*" he said.

Suddenly, they were both laughing.

"So what are we going to do?" she asked.

"I think we should leave."

"We just got here."

"How can we stay?"

"How can we leave?" Emily said. "We're both naked. Our clothes are in there."

"Our suitcases are in the car. We can change."

"You mean, just forget about the squirrel?"

"What choice do we have? Where are the car keys?"

"I left them in the car with my purse."

"Good," said Joel. "Let's go."

Naked as newborn babes, they left the house. Fortunately, it was pitch-dark outside. Emily retrieved the car key from her purse on the front seat and unlocked the trunk. They each opened their overnight bags, grabbed some underwear and whatever else they could find to cover themselves, and got dressed. They had no shoes, but that didn't seem important. They could ride back to the city shoeless. Joel had only one pair of jeans, and they were in the bedroom with the squirrel, so he wore only boxer shorts.

"Can you drive?" asked Emily. "I'm too exhausted."

"Sure," said Joel. He got behind the wheel, started the motor, and drove off, down the driveway and back onto the Taconic.

After a few moments, Emily, reflective, said, "I guess I'll have some explaining to do to my aunt."

"Do you think the squirrel will be dead when she comes back to the house?"

Emily shrugged.

"Do you think she'll give me back my clothes?" asked Joel. "They're my favorite jeans."

Emily laughed.

"Are you hungry?" he asked.

"I guess so."

"I'm starved."

"Can you wait till we get back to the city?"

"I suppose."

"There's a nice little restaurant a few blocks from my apartment."

"Good. Do you think they'll mind that I'm in my underwear?"

"Oops," she said. "We better go directly to my place, and I'll make some eggs or something. That's about all I have in the refrigerator."

"Eggs would be fine," he said.

"Maybe some bread and butter and some milk." She moved closer to him. They rode in silence for a short while.

"Could you put your hand between my legs again like before?" he asked. "It felt so nice."

"Do you think that's safe while your driving?"

"If I don't pay any attention, it'll be perfectly safe."

"Oh, okay," said Emily.

She stroked him for a minute or two, felt his hardness, and said, "You're paying attention."

"I am?" said Joel.

"I think I'm in love with you."

"The feeling is mutual."

They were married the following year.

Lou's Death

In 1969, it became clear to the Sachs family that something was wrong with Lou. He started losing weight for the first time in his life, he was constantly fatigued, and his vision was blurred. They urged him to see Dr. Hines, the family doctor, but he refused.

"I don't believe in throwing away money on doctors," he said. "All they know is pills and cutting you open. Leave me alone with doctors."

He was so adamant about it that at first the family gave in. But soon there were days when he didn't have the energy to get out of bed and go to work or even eat. He looked like hell. Still, he refused to see the doctor, so Rose phoned Joel and told him she was at her wit's end and needed his help. Joel called Dr. Hines and told him what was going on. Hines told Joel to get Lou to the emergency room at Bronx Hospital immediately.

"I'll call ahead and tell them to expect you, and I'll tell them I want a complete work-up. I'll call you as soon as I get the results."

Joel called Gloria, Lou's favorite child, to ask for her assistance in getting their father to the E.R. Gloria showed up immediately.

"An emergency room?" Lou asked Joel and Gloria. "Are you crazy? What's the emergency?"

Joel said, "Dr. Hines wants you to have some tests so he can figure out what's wrong with you. He says it sounds serious."

"Dr. Hines is an idiot," said Lou. "I work too hard, that's all."

"Rose called out from the next room, "Dr. Hines is not an idiot. *You're* the idiot!"

"Who asked you?" Lou called back, but his voice was very weak.

Gloria, in tears, begged Lou to go for the tests. "For my sake, Daddy, please."

Her tears did it. From the time she was a child, whenever she cried, Lou melted.

He went with Joel and Gloria to Bronx Hospital, sat with them in the waiting room for three hours, cursed the hospital for the long wait, and kept threatening to leave if they didn't call his name soon. But he stayed.

When the phlebotomist finally called him, she tied a tourniquet around his upper arm and said, "This may hurt a little." Then she pricked his artery with a needle.

"Ow!" shrieked Lou. "You clumsy cow!"

"Dad," Joel scolded, "for God's sake…!"

"Well, she hurt me," said Lou.

"You should have more respect," said the phlebotomist.

"Respect for what?" asked Lou.

"For me," she answered.

"You kept me waiting three hours, and you practically killed me with that needle. Where'd you get your license?"

"Daddy, please," Gloria begged. "Be nice."

When the phlebotomist was finished, she said, "Good riddance, Mr. Sachs."

On the way out of the hospital, Lou grumbled that "the whole thing was a big waste of time," just as he knew it would be.

*   *   *

A few days later, Dr. Hines called and told Joel to bring his father into the office as soon as possible. Emily wished him luck as he left.

"If he gives me a hard time," said Joel, "I'll just tie him up and drag him out by the rope."

When he arrived at his parents' apartment, they were in their bedroom, arguing. Lou was sitting fully dressed on the edge of their bed. "Come on," said Rose. "Joel's here."

"I told you, I'm not going."

"And I'm telling you, you *are* going."

"Let's go, Dad," said Joel. "Be a good boy."

"I'm not going to any doctor. I haven't been in a doctor's office since my bar mitzvah, and I'm not starting now."

"Put your coat on," said Joel.

"Don't boss me around," said Lou.

"Do you want to die, Lou? Is that what you want?" asked Rose. Not that she loved Lou—she hadn't been in love with him since before Gloria was born, and Gloria was now twenty-two. But he was her husband, and she felt it her duty to take the best possible care of him.

"I want everyone to leave me alone, that's what I want."

"Forget it, Dad. We're not leaving you alone," said Joel.

"You have to go," said Rose. "Gloria and Fanny are meeting us there. Your kids took the day off for you."

"Remind me to give them medals."

"Come on," said Joel, and he took Lou gently by the arm and lifted him up from the bed. "You may have lost weight," said Joel in an attempt to lighten the situation, "but you're still pretty heavy."

Lou pulled his arm away from Joel. "Who needs your help?"

Reluctantly, he followed Rose out of the bedroom, but when he lost his balance and almost toppled over, he changed his mind and took Joel's arm.

On the street, Joel hailed a taxi.

"What's wrong with the subway?" asked Lou.

Joel ignored him.

A taxi pulled up. Joel opened the back door and helped Lou in first, then Rose.

"Who can afford a cab?" said Lou.

"It's my treat," said Joel. "163rd Street and the Grand Concourse," Joel told the driver, and got in beside Rose.

"When did you become a rich man?" Lou asked his son.

"Once and for all, close your mouth and don't say another word," Rose commanded.

"Button your lip, lady. No woman bosses Lou Sachs around."

Up front, the taxi driver chuckled.

When they entered Dr. Hines' office, Fanny and Gloria had already arrived.

"Why are the two of you here?" Lou asked, irritated. "I feel like this is my funeral."

"We're here because we love you," said Gloria, and gave him a kiss.

Fanny did not kiss him.

The receptionist said that Dr. Hines was waiting for Lou. "Only two family members are permitted to accompany him into the examining room."

"Why only two?" asked Lou.

"We don't want the room to be overcrowded, now do we?" replied the receptionist.

It was decided that Fanny and Gloria would remain in the

waiting room.

Dr. Hines appeared, greeted the family, and led Lou, Rose, and Joel inside.

Fanny skimmed a magazine. "I don't know what I'm doing here."

"Our father is very sick," said Gloria, too worried to do anything but fret, "that's what you're doing here."

"You think *he'd* be here if *I* was the one who was sick?" asked Fanny.

"Of course he would."

"Take off the rose-colored glasses, little sister."

Gloria grabbed a magazine and pretended to read. She and Fanny waited in silence.

"Before we go any further," Dr. Hines said to Lou, "I have two questions for you. First, why are you fifty pounds overweight?"

Rose was shocked. "Fifty pounds? It's not possible. He doesn't eat a thing."

"I'd like Lou to answer my questions, Rose," said the doctor. "The second question, why haven't you come in for a check-up in all these years?"

"I didn't see the point," answered Lou.

"The point is, we might have caught your diabetes earlier, which could have meant a less serious case and threat to your life."

Rose turned white as a sheet. "Diabetes?"

"Type 2," said Dr. Hines. "The worst kind."

"God in heaven!" said Rose, dotting her perspiring forehead with a tissue.

The doctor said, "Too much fat, too much sugar, too many carbohydrates."

Lou said, "I like to eat. It makes me happy. I'm fat, so what?"

"So you're a very sick man with a very dangerous disease. People with diabetes often have big problems: hyperglycemic hyperosmolar nonketotic syndrome, for example."

"Speak English," said Lou.

Dr. Hines clarified: "Diabetic coma, cold sweats, trembling hands, intense anxiety, a general sense of confusion, and"—the doctor emphasized—"a risk of heart disease and an increased risk of stroke and glaucoma, which can lead to blindness."

"If you're trying to scare me, Doctor," said Lou, "look." He held his hands out. "I'm not shaking."

"*I* am," said Rose. "I'm shaking like a leaf!"

"See if *this* scares you, Lou," said the doctor. "Diabetes can slow down your body's ability to fight infection. High blood sugar leads to high levels of sugar in your body's tissues, allowing bacteria to grow and infections to develop more quickly. You can wind up with gangrene and no legs."

"Stop talking like a doctor already," said Lou, who by now was very frightened, although he wouldn't admit it.

"In plain English," said the doctor, "you've done a lot of damage to your body. You'll be required to give yourself insulin shots in your thigh twice a day—without fail."

"Shots?"

"Correct," said the doctor.

"To *myself*?"

"Correct."

"I hate needles."

"You better get to like them. And you'll have to do a lot of exercise," the doctor continued, "walking and running and stretching, and go on a controlled diet if you want to go on living."

"No diet," said Lou, "and no exercise. Maybe I'll shoot

myself in my thigh once in a while, but that's all I'll do."

"Not good enough," said the doctor. "If you don't do everything I tell you, I don't want you as my patient. I believe in saving lives, not watching my patients commit suicide."

"Fine," said Lou. And to Rose and Joel he said, "Let's go."

Ignoring Lou, Joel asked the doctor, "What exactly is the diet? Is it very strict?"

"He'll have to eat foods low in fat to keep the risk of heart disease as limited as possible. He'll have to avoid fat calories, which can help him lose excess weight, especially when combined with an exercise program."

"No exercise, I told you," said Lou.

Again ignoring Lou, Joel asked, "What foods specifically should he avoid?"

"Cheese, beef, milk, and baked goods. Also fats in vegetables oils are harder. We recognize these as solid oils. Many of them are used in baking and frying."

This worried Rose. "You mean I can't bake or fry anymore?"

"Not for your husband," said the doctor.

"That's all he eats," said Rose. "Hamburgers in Crisco!"

"Not anymore," said Dr. Hines.

"Ridiculous!" said Lou.

"*You're* ridiculous," said Joel. "Just listen to Dr. Hines and don't interrupt."

"Who do you think you're talking to, Mister?" said Lou.

"To a *baby*," said Joel.

"Watch your mouth."

Doctor Hines, noting that Joel seemed to be the sanest one in the room, handed him a sheet of paper. "Here are some general guidelines for selecting and preparing low-fat foods for a Type 2 diabetes diet."

Joel read aloud from the paper: "One: Select low-fat foods

including poultry, fish, lean red meats, and plant-based proteins. When preparing these foods, don't fry them. Instead, you can bake, broil, grill, roast, or boil."

Rose moaned. "He won't eat them."

"That's right," said Lou and crossed his arms for emphasis.

"He has to learn to eat a healthy diet," said Hines.

Lou brushed away the doctor's words like they were a bothersome fly.

Joel read on: "Two: Select low-fat or nonfat dairy products, such as low-fat cheese, skim milk, and products made from skim milk such as nonfat yogurt, evaporated skim milk, and buttermilk."

Lou interrupted. "Yogurt? Are you kidding me?"

Joel continued. "Remember to include dairy products in your daily carbohydrate count."

"I hate yogurt! I never eat it!" said Lou.

"It's true," said Rose.

Joel went on reading: "Three: Use low-fat vegetable cooking spray when preparing foods."

"Okay, fine," said Lou. "I'll starve myself to death."

"Number four:" Joel continued. "Use liquid vegetable oils that contain poly- or mono-unsaturated fats which can help lower your 'bad' LDL cholesterol. Five: Select lower fat margarines, gravies, and salad dressings and remember to watch the carbohydrate count on condiments and dressings."

"What does it mean—carbohydrate count?" asked Rose, frustrated.

"It's explained in a footnote," said Joel. "You can read it when you get home. Six: All fruits and vegetables are good low-fat choices. Remember to include fruit and starchy vegetables in your daily carbohydrate count."

"Fruit I like," said Lou. "And starchy also."

"That's it," said Joel. "That's the diet."

I'll give you the name of a registered dietitian who can provide more information on how to prepare and select low-fat foods," the doctor said. "I want to see you back here in a month."

"I can't wait," said Lou.

Lou, seated between Gloria and Rose in the back seat, spent the entire taxi ride home grousing. "I never should have listened to you. Thirty-five dollars for a useless check-up! Plus cab fare!"

"It wasn't useless, Daddy," said Gloria. "You have a bad disease. You really have to start taking care of yourself."

"If he wants to die," said Fanny, seated in one of the two jump seats, "let him. Who'll miss him?"

"I will," said Gloria.

"I won't," said Fanny. "With his gambling and his shylocks, he's probably better off dead."

Lou was too exhausted to defend himself. It was Joel, sitting on the second jump seat, who lost his temper and shouted at Fanny, "Once and for all, will you shut your trap?"

Everyone was shocked, Fanny most of all.

"Good for you, Joel," said Gloria.

"You see?" said Fanny. "Everyone in this family hates me."

"Can you blame us?" Gloria asked. "You don't have a drop of compassion—except for yourself! Can't you find an ounce for your own father?"

If hair could actually stand up on a person's head, Fanny's would have reached the roof of the taxi at Gloria's words.

"Listen, Miss Fatty Sachs," she said, "and listen good. And you, too, Mr. Goody-Goody Joel Sachs. I'm older than both of

141

you, and you're not allowed to talk to me like that. I'm sick of being criticized by *children*!"

"Be nice to each other," said Rose. "We're a family. In a family, people are supposed to be nice to each other."

"Since when?" asked Fanny. "The four of you may be a family, but I'm not part of it. I never have been."

Rose ignored her and turned to Joel. "What am I supposed to feed him if I can't fry his hamburgers in Crisco?"

"It isn't necessary to *fry* hamburgers, Ma. You can broil them. Emily never fries anything except an egg once in a while."

"Emily?" said Lou with a sneer. "She's a rotten cook! I remember her food at your wedding. It was from hunger. Anyway, who ever heard of a bride cooking the food for her own wedding?"

"What are you talking about, Daddy?" said Gloria. "Emily's a great cook."

"I still say her parents should have hired a caterer," said Lou. "I never heard of a wedding without a caterer."

"You didn't even give me a wedding," said Fanny, "so what are you carrying on about? You refused to lay out a penny!"

"If I was the richest person in the United States, I wouldn't pay for anything that has to do with Harvey. As far as I'm concerned, he's not worth a penny."

"That's a nice way to talk about my husband," said Fanny.

"He's nasty to everybody, isn't he? He calls everybody in this family nasty names, doesn't he? Including *you*."

"Maybe if you treated him better, he'd be nicer to you. He feels like an outsider, the way I do."

"What about his own family?" asked Lou. "Is he nice to *them*?"

"They give him about as much love as my family gives me."

"Does he hit them, too?" asked Rose.

"What?" asked Fanny, almost jumping out of her seat. "What do you mean?"

"He hits you, doesn't he?"

"Who told you that?"

"Nobody has to tell me," said Rose. "I've seen the bruises on you."

"He hits her?" asked Lou. "That piece of garbage hits my daughter?"

"Is that true, Fanny?" asked Joel. "Does Harvey hit you?"

"You should keep your mouth shut, Ma," said Fanny.

"When *you* shut your mouth, I'll shut *mine*."

"Is it true, Fanny?" Joel repeated.

"We hit each other," said Fanny. "I get my shots in too, believe me."

"You live with a man who hits you?" asked Gloria.

"At least he has a job. At least he makes a good living. He's not a loser like your boyfriend!"

"Ralph is not my boyfriend anymore."

"I never liked him," said Rose. "I begged you to get rid of him."

"I did get rid of him," said Gloria. "My boyfriend now is Raymond, and he has a very good job."

"Maybe Harvey hits his parents, too," Rose said. "Maybe that's why they refused to pay for your wedding."

"They wouldn't pay for it because they felt the bride's parents should pay for the wedding," said Fanny.

"Cheap bastards!" said Lou.

"What about *you*? You're not cheap? We had to elope and get married by a justice of the peace at our own expense because of how cheap you are!"

"Do we have to carry on like this?" asked Gloria. "We just

found out that Daddy has diabetes. Why are we reviewing all this depressing history?"

Lou yawned. "I just wanna sleep," he said.

"You used to give that Ralph money, didn't you?" Rose asked Gloria.

"What?" said Lou. "You gave him money?"

"I made a mistake, I admit it," said Gloria.

"I was so surprised at you," said Rose.

"I wasn't," said Fanny. "I always said Gloria was a jerk."

"She was just young," said Joel.

"I like Raymond, though," said Rose. "He reminds me of Joel. *A mensch.* But that Ralph: he was almost as bad as Harvey."

"Nobody's as bad as Harvey," said Lou.

"What am I doing in this taxi?" said Fanny. "All I get from this family are insults. Driver, pull over and let me off."

"Don't be ridiculous," said Rose. "You're coming back to the apartment for lunch. I made a delicious cabbage soup last night."

"Cabbage soup gives me gas," said Fanny.

"Should I pull over or not?" asked the driver.

"Or not," said Rose.

They heard a snore. Lou was fast asleep.

"Poor Daddy's worn out," said Gloria.

The conversation was over for now.

One day, two years later, Lou forgot that he'd already taken his insulin that morning, injected himself in the thigh a second time, and wound up in the emergency room of Lincoln Hospital suffering from insulin shock. A young intern managed to save his life. Afterwards, Joel, Emily, Gloria, and Rose pleaded with him to change his diet and get some exercise, but he told them all, "Go to hell and mind your business. It's *my* life. I'll live the way I want until I die." Gloria's pleas and tears made no difference this time.

Within four years, Dr. Hines saw signs of gangrene and warned Lou that he was on his way to losing a leg.

Lou told the doctor, "I'm not losing any legs. Get off my back." He swore from then on never to see any doctor again. The following year, Lou's left leg was amputated from the knee down, and he spent the rest of his life on crutches or in a wheelchair.

In the last year of his life, he had a stroke. He lost the ability to speak and all feeling on the left side of his body. He was in Bronx Hospital for two months and when he made no progress, stopped eating and lost almost 100 pounds, the hospital refused to keep him and told the family he had to be moved into a nursing home.

In the nursing home, not far from where Rose now lived alone, there was no improvement. Lou didn't regain his speech or any movement on the left side of his body. He was mostly restricted to bed or to a wheelchair. When nurses fed him pills, he would take them into his mouth and pretend to swallow them, but when nobody was looking, he'd spit them out. Rose, Gloria, and Joel took turns going to the nursing home to feed him, but he couldn't or wouldn't eat. A few times with his right arm he knocked the tray onto the floor and sometimes into Rose's lap, soiling her dress. He was incontinent, but the nurses were so overworked that he would usually have to wait hours, sitting or lying in his own waste, before anyone came to clean him up. Over and over, he tried telling each family visitor something that seemed urgent to him, but all that emerged from his voicebox was one word that sounded like "gofee."

"Gofee, Daddy? Is that what you're saying?" Gloria asked.

Lou shook his head, which the family had come to realize meant "yes." When his answer was "no," he nodded his head.

"Go free?" asked Joel. "Are you asking to 'go free'"?

Lou nodded his head.

"Coffee?" asked Rose. "You want some coffee, Lou?"

He groaned in frustration and nodded his head.

"You're slurring your words, Daddy," Gloria said. "We can't understand you." Lou wept. His tears were so painful to Gloria that she wept with him.

One day when none of the others was there, Fanny showed up with Harvey. When Lou saw them, he shocked them by sitting up sharply in the hospital bed and waving his right fist threateningly first at Fanny, then at Harvey, and growling at them so menacingly that an orderly had to come over to calm him down.

Fanny was hysterical. "He hates me!" she cried. "He's always hated me. All my life!"

Harvey took her by the hand and pulled her away towards the elevator. "Don't pay any attention to him. He's not in his right mind."

Fanny turned and shouted at Lou, "This is the last time you'll ever see me, old man!"

She kept her promise. By the end of the year, her father was dead.

The family—minus Fanny and Harvey—was brought into the funeral after the mourners had been seated. Gloria entered first with Raymond, his arm around her. She was shedding heavy tears. As Rose entered, she lost all control. She rushed at the closed coffin, banged on it with her fists, and stomped her feet, crying, "Lou, don't die! Don't die! Don't leave me alone!"

Her dress flew up over her hips, revealing her underwear and the garters that held her stockings up. There were gasps of shock throughout the chapel. Joel rushed at his mother, put his arm around her, drew her tightly to him, and said to her in an angry whisper, "Stop it, Ma. Enough performing!" She pulled herself together.

After Lou's casket had been interred and the *Kaddish* read, the assembled group began to depart. Joel, who up to that point had not felt much, whispered something to Emily, let go of her hand, and walked alone over the vast cemetery grounds.

He stopped under a tree and, looking down, closed his eyes. "Gofee," he muttered and then began to sob. He wasn't sure why.

For the duration of the mourning period, Joel, Emily, Gloria, and Raymond moved in with Rose, despite her assurances that she was all right on her own. They covered all the mirrors and, except for meals, sat shoeless on wooden boxes. Friends and family visited and brought food and cookies and cakes, expressed their sympathy, and shared memories of Lou. Fanny and Harvey did not show up. Rose said she would never forgive Fanny as long as she lived. What kind of daughter would ignore her father's death? Rose was convinced once and for all that Fanny was completely heartless.

As the days passed and the visitors had come and gone, the family found it more and more difficult to think of favorable things to say about Lou. Gloria remembered a few happy and amusing moments she had shared with him—good times they'd spent together going to the deli every Sunday for hotdogs and french fries, to Coney Island, to the movies, watching TV, and reading together.

"You're lucky," said Rose. "Most of what I remember is his gambling and the fights we had."

Emily was surprised. "That's all you remember?"

"Well," said Rose, "I also remember when I realized he was the one who broke the bank Joelly loved so much and stole the money in it."

"What?" said Joel. "Did you just say what I think you said, Ma?"

"Daddy's the one who broke Joel's bank?" asked Gloria, as shocked as Joel. "Is that what you're saying?"

"Yes," said Rose. "I said it was the colored girl, but it was Daddy. I even fired her."

"I don't believe it," said Gloria.

"You think I would lie about something like that?"

"But he made the bank himself," said Joel. "With his own two hands."

"That's right," said Rose.

"Why would he destroy something he made for me? He was so proud of it."

"He needed the money to pay off a shylock," said Rose.

"Oh, God!" said Gloria, devastated. "How pathetic!"

"It never occurred to me that he was a thief," said Joel.

Rose shrugged. "That's a gambler for you. Period. End of story."

Let's Make a Baby

In the tenth year of their marriage, when Emily was thirty-six and Joel thirty-seven, they went to see a fertility specialist to find out why Emily wasn't able to conceive. Her gynecologist had assured her that nothing was wrong with her reproductive system, and urged her to see a psychiatrist just in case there was something emotional or psychological that was preventing conception. What Emily and the psychiatrist, Dr. Mallory, determined was that, if there was a problem, it was that Emily's biggest dream wasn't coming true. All her life, she had prepared to be a mother, and she still didn't have her child. It was all the more stressful because every day at work she faced a classroom of thirty or more children. She adored them, but their only connection to her was as a teacher, and after fifteen years, Emily wanted a closer bond. Dr. Mallory advised her to consider the possibility that the issue might be Joel's, not hers. He recommended that together they see a specialist to find out if Joel's sperm were healthy.

Emily struggled with the notion of suggesting this to Joel. A few of her female friends had told her that for some men, the ability to make a baby was a metaphor for manhood. As much as she trusted that Joel was not that shallow, it worried her that she might in some way diminish him by suggesting that the problem could be his. She adored Joel as much now as she had when they first traveled together to Aunt Grace's house in Putnam Valley and run away from a squirrel in the middle of very hot sex. She knew he felt the same way about her. They had a satisfying life together: they enjoyed the same things, had plenty of good friends and a decent apartment in Manhattan that they both loved. As far as she was concerned, everything about their marriage was ideal—except that their lifelong mutual dream of being parents had not come true. And her biological clock was ticking away.

One evening at dinner, Emily was watching Joel eat with his usual relish as he told her about his day. A student in his English-novel course had insisted that Thomas Hardy's *Return of the Native* was second-rate and a waste of time. This provoked a spirited argument in the class, with some students joining with Joel in defending one of the great novelists of all time. It was terrific fun, and Joel's joy in the experience and in telling her about it gave Emily the courage and confidence she was looking for. She told him what Dr. Mallory had advised.

Joel was startled. He had never thought about the possibility that he was the one with the fertility problem.

"He thinks my sperm may be the issue?"

"He didn't say that. He just said that if we're anxious to have a child, we should do everything possible to find out what's preventing it. He said there's a clinic on the Upper East Side, the Muller Clinic, with fertility doctors who can do a simple test to examine your sperm. He said the clinic has a very good reputation and a high success rate helping women conceive."

"What would I have to do?" Joel asked.

"I don't really know. Why don't we go and find out?"

Joel stopped eating and sat silent for a while.

Emily felt a slight panic. "We don't have to if you don't want to," she said. "I mean, it's just that I've presented us to Dr.

Mallory as pretty desperate to have a family, and because of my age and all..."

"I understand," said Joel. "Let's make an appointment tomorrow."

Emily beamed. "Oh, Joel!" She got up and went over to him. She sat on his lap. She smiled at him. "You're such a *mensch*."

"Don't make so much of it," said Joel. "I don't really want to go through with it. I'm doing it for you...and your shrink."

"I'm very grateful," said Emily, and she kissed him.

That night, Joel didn't sleep. "What if?" kept going through his mind. And each time the question came into his head, he became more and more uneasy. At about 4 A.M., he woke Emily and repeated the question to her: "What if?"

"You mean what if the problem is yours?"

"Yes," said Joel with an edge of hostility.

"We'll deal with it, that's all."

"How?"

"Let's not go there yet, Joel. Let's wait and find out."

"But I can't sleep."

"Do you want a tranquilizer?"

"No. What I want is to get it over with."

"Lie closer to me," said Emily. "I'll stroke your head. That will relax you."

At 6 A.M. Joel finally fell asleep.

At 7:30, the alarm went off.

At 8, Emily called the Muller Clinic and made an appointment for 4 P.M. She suggested to Joel that they meet there after school.

When they left the apartment at 8:30 to travel to their respective jobs—she in her car, he on the bus—Joel said goodbye abruptly and did not kiss Emily. She decided not to make a thing of it because she understood the pressure he was feeling. She felt the same way every time she went to her gynecologist.

Joel was not his usual self at school. He was short-tempered and impatient with his students. When school was out, he considered not going to the clinic and making up some excuse: the bus broke down, I forgot the address, I got lost. In the end, he hailed a taxi and waited for Emily outside the clinic for a half-hour.

She smiled when she saw him. He looked grim.

"I didn't expect you to get here before me," said Emily.

"I don't know what I'm doing here," he said.

She took his hand and led him inside.

The waiting room was so crowded with patients of all ages that there were no seats available. Emily pointed out to Joel the large number of men and women their age and even younger who were obviously in their same situation.

The receptionist greeted them, handed them some forms to fill out, and told them they'd be seeing Dr. Lampell, one of the three clinic doctors. Joel remarked that it would be difficult filling out a form without a place to sit. The receptionist apologized for the shortage of seats and suggested they use the window ledge as a desk. Joel grumbled all through the process of filling out the forms. "Why do they have to know our incomes?" "What business is it of theirs how often we have sex?" "Why is it important what our hobbies are?"

Emily was silent, careful not to engage with him given his mood. But Joel wanted an argument. He wanted to spew out the anger he felt.

"Doesn't it upset you?" he asked.

"As far as I'm concerned," said Emily, "it's no big deal."

"Well, I happen to resent the invasion of privacy," said Joel.

"If it gets us a baby," said Emily, "it will have been worth it."

Emily got a seat when a woman nearby was called into one of the examining rooms. Another woman, in the seat to next to Emily, turned to her and asked, "Is this your first time?"

"Is it that obvious?" asked Emily.

"I wish I could tell you you're in for a pleasant time. You see this?" The woman held up a small jar of white liquid. "My husband's contribution. It's three hours old—that's how long I've been waiting. What are the odds that any of his sperm are still alive?"

"Three hours?" Emily asked.

"I've waited as long as four hours some days."

"Oh, wow," said Emily. "How can they have a high success rate?"

"They say they do, but who knows what the truth is? It's a business, after all." She pointed to Joel. "That's your husband, huh?"

"Yes," said Emily.

"He doesn't look too happy. It must be *his* problem, huh?"

"That's what we're here to find out," said Emily.

At that moment, the receptionist called, "Mr. and Mrs. Sachs?"

Emily raised her hand. "Here," she said, as if she were one of her own pupils responding to the roll call.

"Room 4," said the receptionist.

Emily got up and Joel joined her.

"Lampell's the worst," said the woman Emily had been talking to.

Fearful that Joel, hearing this, might turn around and leave, Emily led him by the hand into Room 4. As they entered Lampell's office, Joel whispered to Emily, "'The worst,' huh?"

"Oh," said Emily, "She's just a doom-and-gloomer."
Dr. Maurice Lampell was sitting behind his desk, reading their medical history. Without looking up or saying a word, he signaled with his hand for Joel and Emily to sit down. During the interview that followed, the doctor rarely looked up, and when he did it was to glance out the window. He had lost much of his hair, so most of the time they were looking at his bald head. Whenever he glanced up, his glasses had slipped halfway down his nose, and he looked over the top of the frames. He paid so little attention to them that it wasn't clear if he would recognize them five minutes after they left his office.

"I see you've had quite a few childhood diseases, Mr. Sachs, including mumps," he said, his eyes directed at Joel's history.

"Yes," said Joel.

"That could explain weak sperm," said the doctor, "which of course makes procreation difficult, if not impossible."

"But we don't know for sure that my sperm are weak, do we, Doctor?" asked Joel.

"I'd bet on it," said Lampell.

This was not a promising beginning. The doctor's assumption that Joel's sperm were weak and that mumps might have been the cause produced a strong feeling of guilt in Joel.

"We've had some success with cases like yours, but they're rare."

"Don't you think you should know for sure whether my sperm are weak before you jump to any conclusions?" asked Joel.

The doctor opened a drawer of his desk, took out a small empty jar, and handed it to Joel.

"Why don't you go into the men's room and produce a semen sample for me. Then I'll take a look under the microscope and determine what's what."

"Are you telling me to masturbate?" asked Joel.

"Do you have a better suggestion?" asked the doctor.

"You expect me to go into a public men's room and...?"

"It's not public. Only one man at a time uses it. And it's very clean."

"Can't I do it at home," asked Joel, "in the privacy of my own bathroom?"

"Don't you want to get this over with so we can move along and try to get your wife pregnant?"

Joel looked at Emily. She felt terrible, both sympathetic and guilt-ridden. "Would you rather forget about the whole thing, darling?" she asked.

"Yes, I would," said Joel. "But I want us to have a baby."

"The men's room is next door," said Lampell, "with a pile of *Playboys* to assist you."

"*Playboy?*" Joel asked, surprised.

"Do you have some objection to *Playboy?*"

"I've never found *Playboy* particularly stimulating."

Lampell looked at Joel directly for once. "Naked women don't arouse you?"

"*Pictures* aren't generally what I use for arousal."

He looked away. "Well, I'm afraid we can't supply naked women in the flesh."

"Frankly, Dr. Lampell," said Joel, "I find the notion of going into a clinic restroom to masturbate—with or without 'assistance' from magazines—repellent."

"You don't have to stay on my account, Mr. Sachs," said the doctor. "You have my permission to leave."

With an obvious edge of anger, Joel stood up, holding the jar, and turned towards the door. "I'll be back—eventually," he said.

"Take your time", said Lampell. "In the meantime, I'll talk to your wife."

*   *   *

With a good many eyes in the waiting room watching him, Joel found the men's room and disappeared inside. On the door of a cabinet under the washstand was a sign: *Magazines*. With a grunt, Joel opened the cabinet door and grabbed a few *Playboys* off the top of the stack. He put them on the floor next to the toilet. He washed his hands, took down his pants and underpants, uncapped the jar and set it on the floor, sat down on the toilet seat, and, leafing through the first of the magazines, strained to get himself erect.

In Lampell's office, the doctor told Emily about the procedure he would recommend if it turned out, as he believed, that Joel's sperm count was low. "If you choose to proceed, I'll give you your first shot of Clomid today. Clomid is used to guarantee that you ovulate approximately on schedule. Make use of a basal thermometer, and when you see a rise in your temperature, that's the sign that you're ovulating."

"Yes," said Emily, "I know that. I've been using a basal thermometer for years."

"Good. On your first day of ovulation, call here and tell the receptionist you're coming in for an insemination."

"With my husband?" asked Emily.

"Well, yes," said Lampell. "Unless you have another source for producing semen."

"Can't he produce it at home? He'll be a lot more relaxed and comfortable about the whole procedure."

"It's a lot better if it's inseminated when it's fresh. And it's freshest if it's produced a short time before it's inseminated."

Meanwhile, Joel had been in the men's room for after fifteen minutes with no results. Then he came upon a photo in the second *Playboy* of a faceless woman—her head had been cropped out of the photo— lying on her back, totally nude, her legs spread apart, the middle finger of her right hand stuck in her vagina. This picture did the trick. In about three minutes, Joel ejaculated into the jar. He took a few seconds to catch his breath then returned the *Playboy* to the stack, capped the jar, pulled himself together, and left the bathroom carrying his produce. As he emerged, dozens of eyes were on him in the waiting room. He moved quickly, jar in hand, to Lampell's office.

"Are you okay?" asked Emily.

"I'm fine," said Joel.

"It wasn't so bad, was it?" asked Lampell.

"No," said Joel, "it was terrific. I think it may be my favorite way to have sex from now on."

Dr. Lampell poured some of Joel's fresh semen onto a slide and placed it under the lens of the microscope on his desk. Emily and Joel sat silent and tense, as the doctor peered into the microscope. "Aha!" he said, after a minute or so. "Just as I suspected. Double-tail sperm."

"What does that mean?" asked Joel.

"It's not good," said the doctor. "Come over here and take a look."

Reluctantly, Joel went behind the desk and looked into the microscope.

"Notice," said Lampell, "that every now and then there's a normal sperm. Not too many, but then again it only takes one to connect with your wife's egg and make a baby. It won't be easy and it may take a while."

"But you think you can help us?" said Emily.

"I'm willing to try if you are," said the doctor.

"Well, I know I am," said Emily, and she looked at Joel, who seemed devastated.

"A 'few' healthy sperm?" he asked the doctor.

"A very few," said Lampell.

"What are our chances?" asked Joel.

"Limited," said the doctor.

"How limited?"

"Based on my experience, *very* limited."

"Shit!" said Joel. He sat down in his chair, put his head into his hands, and did what he could not to cry.

Emily rubbed his back. "Maybe we'll be lucky," she said.

"Maybe not," said Joel. "Maybe we shouldn't go any further, just to find out we're not going to have a family."

"Oh, Joel, don't be so pessimistic. Please."

Dr. Lampell cleared his throat and said, "I have other patients waiting. Why don't the two of you go home, talk it over, and let me know what you decide."

Joel got up and left the room, and Emily, who could not control her tears, followed him out. When they reached the street, Joel turned to her and said, "Where are you parked?

"Joel…" she said, trying to comfort him.

He interrupted her. "I don't want to talk. I've heard enough talk."

Emily said nothing more. She led him to her car. They drove home in silence.

When they entered their apartment, Joel went into the living room and sat down.

"Do you want to be alone or do you want to talk now?" asked Emily.

"I don't want to go any further with this," said Joel.

"Oh," said Emily.

"I can't take it. It's that simple."

She went over to him, leaned down, and kissed him. "I'll start dinner." She went off the to the kitchen.

Joel sat alone and stewed.

*   *   *

Over dinner, Emily suggested that they could both use a rest and a change of scene, and since they had over a week before the new school term began, they should take a brief vacation.

"I say we get into the car and just drive north. Maybe to Maine. Mount Desert Island. We had such a lovely time last year. Clam chowder. Lobsters. Blueberry pie. Hikes. Cool weather. What do you think?"

Joel was surprised at how accepting she seemed of what had to be a great disappointment. "How come you aren't that upset?" he asked. "Is it an act or are you really that cool with it?"

"I'm not sure," she said. "I just think we should get away for a while and maybe gain a new perspective."

They left the very next morning.

The trip started well enough. They played Twenty Questions and laughed a lot, then they sang along with the Beatles, Barbra Streisand, and Sonny and Cher. In Joel's opinion, Emily had a "fantastic" voice. In Emily's opinion, Joel's voice was "pleasant enough." The weather was perfect: smog-free blue skies, whipped-cream clouds, a bright but not too hot sun, and cool, crisp air. Joel assumed they were headed for a glorious trip. As they approached New Hampshire later in the day, he asked Emily if she wanted to stop for lunch. Suddenly, she burst into deep sobs. Joel was thrown. He asked her what was wrong, but she couldn't speak, she could only cry and blow her nose into a tissue. He left the road and pulled into a parking area at a gas station at the bottom of the off-ramp, turned off the motor, and tried to take her hand. She pulled it away.

"What is it?" he asked.

She spent at least a minute getting a grip on herself. When she could finally stop crying, she took a deep breath and blurted out, "I want a baby!"

Joel said nothing. What could he say? He blamed himself for not being able to give her a child, but what could he do? Apologize? Wallow in guilt? Take his life?

"Everyone we know has children," said Emily. "Gloria and Raymond have one. Even awful Fanny and hideous Harvey. Our closest friends. Our colleagues at our schools. Your mother and my mother ask me over and over, 'So when already?' 'Isn't it time?' 'How long are you going to make me wait?' 'Soon it'll be too late.' And they're right: I'm almost too old."

"I know it's my fault, Emily…"

Emily cut him off. "It's not about *fault*. I'm not looking to place the blame. I just want to get pregnant. We'd be such good parents. We'd have a terrific kid. It would be so wanted and so loved. I don't want to be deprived of that, Joel. I want us to go through with insemination. I want to go back to the clinic and see it through. I don't know any other way."

"In other words, you want me to agree to jerk off once a month in the hope that one of my 'very few' single-tailed sperm connects with one of your eggs and produces a child."

"Yes," said Emily. "That's what I want."

"Let's go home," said Joel.

"What?"

"I'll do what you want, but I'm not in the mood for a vacation anymore."

He revved the engine and drove up the ramp back onto the highway. "And don't expect me to come to the clinic with you to jerk off. I'll do it at home, and you can take my sick sperm with you."

Emily said nothing.

"And if that asshole doctor doesn't like it, tell him I said he should go fuck himself."

Emily remained silent.

"If he's the one who inseminates you, I hope he looks between your legs and not at his desk!"

They hardly spoke a word to each other for the rest of the drive home. Emily played some soft music on the radio at a very low volume, which only underscored their sadness.

The next day, Emily drove to the Muller Clinic for her first shot of Clomid.

The following week was the start of school, and both Emily and Joel tried to fill their lives with work. At home, they talked only about their classes, their students, and their colleagues. They both griped a good deal about the inefficiency of their administrators. They kept conversation about fertility and the Muller Clinic to a minimum, but of course it was the most prominent issue on their minds. Emily had discussed the situation with her principal, explaining that one day a month she'd have to be late to class. Her principal, who had four children of his own, was sympathetic and understanding. Her class on that day would be covered by substitutes.

Every morning, Emily took her temperature first thing, and for two weeks it remained the same, as was expected. Fifteen days after her Clomid shot, her temperature rose slightly, and she called the clinic to advise them that she was coming in for an insemination. While she called her school to let them know she'd be late, Joel went into the bathroom and masturbated. Because he and Emily hadn't had sex since their initial visit to the clinic—Dr. Asshole, as Joel referred to Lampell, had suggested that Joel's "few healthy sperm" would be stronger if Joel didn't "waste" any on "routine sex"—he ejaculated quickly into one of the small sterilized jars that Emily had brought from the clinic. When he was finished in the bathroom, Emily quickly showered and dressed, had a few sips of orange juice, and placed the jar of semen into a tightly closed baggie, as if Joel's semen were chicken soup and could be protected for freshness that way.

"Shouldn't you eat something?" Joel called after her.

"I'll grab something on the way to work," she replied.

"Won't you be stronger with some breakfast in you?" he asked.

"Maybe," she answered, "but your sperm won't be." She raced out, got into her car, and drove off.

On his way to school, Joel was preoccupied by guilt for not producing his ejaculate at the clinic and for not accompanying Emily there for support. He also worried that Emily would drive too fast, wind up in an accident, and be killed. Then he would not only not have a child, he would not have a wife.

After lunch, he tried to call her at school, but he was told she hadn't come in that day.

"She said she was feeling horrible and thought it best if she spent the day at home," said the office clerk.

In a panic, Joel called the apartment. When Emily answered, he asked, "What happened?"

Instead of answering with words, Emily broke down and cried.

"What?" asked Joel. "What is it?"

"It was horrible!" said Emily.

"I'll be home as soon as possible."

Joel explained the situation briefly to the headmaster, who was understanding and said, "I'll get someone to take over your classes."

An hour later, Joel found Emily in their apartment, sitting at the kitchen table sipping tea. She looked pale and drawn. Joel went over to her, rubbed her shoulders to comfort her, and kissed the top of her head.

"There was so much traffic," she said, "that it took forever. By the time I arrived, I was sure any healthy sperm were dead. The clinic was so crowded that after an hour, I told the receptionist, 'My husband's sperm are very weak, and if I have to wait much longer, I'm sure they'll all be dead.' She was very sweet and sympathetic, 'but there's nothing I can do,' she said. 'I'm required to call people in turn. No exceptions.' Two hours later, my turn came, and a Dr. Kane helped me on to a table and into stirrups. Then he told me to pull my underwear down. I mentioned to him how long it had been since I left home with your semen, and he frowned. 'In that case, I wouldn't put much faith in this insemination. Try to get here earlier next month.'"

At this point, Emily started crying again.

Joel put his arms around her and promised that from now on he'd go with her to the clinic and masturbate there.

"No," said Emily. "It upsets you so much."

"Forget about me. It's you we have to take care of."

A month later, on the first day of ovulation, Joel and Emily arrived at the clinic by eight in the morning. The clinic wouldn't open until nine, but at least thirty people, some of them couples, were already waiting. Once in the waiting room, despite the early hour, it was almost two hours before they were called. A nurse showed Joel to the men's room, reminded him about the stack of *Playboys* under the washstand, and handed him one of the sterile jars.

"Fill out the label, and bring this with you to the front desk when you're finished," she told him matter-of-factly, as if she were a mother telling her son to brush his teeth.

Joel located the issue of *Playboy* with the faceless woman, which once again did the trick. He ejaculated into the jar and capped it, took a minute to catch his breath, and returned the magazine to the stack. He pulled himself together, washed his hands, combed his hair, and left the bathroom with his semen.

Emily waved to him from her seat as he handed the nurse his jar. She told him to have a seat, then called Emily and led her into a room. Fifteen minutes, later, Emily reappeared, looking happy.

Thereafter, the pattern of their life was the same. On the day of ovulation they raced out of the house and to the clinic. When he was called, Joel went into the men's room, found his copy of *Playboy*, masturbated, ejaculated, brought the jar to the nurse, and waited while one of the three doctors inseminated Emily. Then he and Emily left the clinic, grabbed some breakfast, kissed goodbye, and went to work.

One month short of a year after she started inseminations, Emily missed her period for the first time. After a week of tremendous stress, certain that the blood would come at any moment, she called the clinic and spoke to Dr. Lampell. He advised her to wait until her next period, and if she didn't ovulate, she should come in for a pregnancy test. The month passed with both she and Joel feeling anxious day after day, and without anyone else to talk to about what they were going through. They had decided not to mention anything to their families and friends, afraid of jinxing the pregnancy. Emily did not get her period the following month, so she called the clinic and told the receptionist she'd be coming in. She and Joel both took the day off from work and, too nervous to drive, went to the clinic by taxi. They rode in silence the entire way.

Dr. Lane performed the test. The result was positive. Emily was pregnant.

Their surprise and excitement were such that for a minute they were both speechless. Then Joel embraced Emily and held her close, and they dissolved in tears of joy. Dr. Lane congratulated them and told Emily to come back in a month for a follow-up examination. He prepared her for so-called morning sickness and the general fatigue of pregnancy, urged her to pamper herself, and encouraged Joel to be especially kind and caring during the next seven months. They thanked him with such feeling that it was as if he were the hero who had fathered their child.

They left the clinic into a New York that suddenly appeared like a magical land. The streets seemed to glitter. Pedestrians seemed to be smiling at them, happy for their good news. The car horns and screeching brakes resounded like celebratory music. Emily said over and over again, "I can't believe it. I simply can't believe it."

They passed a French bistro, and Joel led Emily inside. It was not quite eleven in the morning, but he ordered caviar for both and champagne for himself. (Dr. Lane had made a point of telling them that he didn't think it was wise for a pregnant woman to drink alcohol.) He toasted her, he toasted the Muller Clinic, he toasted Dr. Lane, and he toasted their developing embryo, certain it was a girl. They even named her—Molly.

As they approached the subway, they passed a children's furniture shop. In an effort to continue the celebration, they went inside, discussing what they should order and what color scheme they should choose for Molly's room. Joel suggested that just in case Molly turned out to be Max, perhaps they should think in terms of a neutral color, neither pink nor blue. Emily agreed, although she was certain she was carrying a girl.

They bought a yellow crib, a white bassinet and bathinette, yellow curtains, a white chest of drawers, mobiles for the crib, framed illustrations from children's books for the walls, and an entire layette in yellow and white. They took off the rest of the day, went home, and phoned family and friends to report their news. There were screams and tears of joy from Joel's mother, Emily's parents, Gloria and Raymond, and from everyone who knew how much they wanted a child and was so happy for them now that their dream was about to come true.

Two days later, everything they'd purchased arrived, and when they came home from work, they set about arranging Molly's room. Joel had some difficulty figuring out how to put the crib together and then how to hang the curtains, but eventually he accomplished it all and the room was bright and fresh and delightful. As they stood at the doorway and took it in, they couldn't stop smiling, the luckiest and happiest couple in the world.

That night they made passionate love. It was the first time in months, and it was as hot as if they were doing it for the first time. "You're better than *Playboy*," Joel said in the midst of their passion, "and much more satisfying than my right hand." Their laughter brought them to the edge, and they exploded in release.

The next four days were the happiest of their married life. Emily's appetite was enormous. She swore her need for food was physical and real. Joel assured her it was also psychological, because he was eating more than ever too, and "I'm not pregnant or even hungry." Each day after school, their phone rang off the hook with people calling to express their good wishes and to share in their success.

Emily's mother called every evening to check up and make sure her daughter was all right. Joel's mother, Rose, also called, but not to talk to Emily. Instead, she would insist on speaking only to Joel—not about his wife's pregnancy, but about her own aches and pains and gripes and dissatisfaction that nobody was paying enough attention to her.

"After all, Joelly," she would whine, "I'm not getting any younger, and I'm all alone. Don't I deserve some consideration?"

Gloria called to say she knew it was premature to discuss this, but she wanted to be the one to give Emily a baby shower when the time was right.

"But you're in Chicago," said Emily. Gloria and Raymond had moved the year before when Gloria had accepted a job at a well-known law firm there.

"That doesn't matter," said Gloria. "I'll come to New York a few days before, and we can plan the event together. Can we do it in your apartment?"

"Sure," said Emily, overwhelmed by how real this whole experience was becoming. She was realizing, with growing excitement, that soon there would be a human being in her arms, and she would be a mother.

Joel had always insisted that he did not believe in God or any other higher power and that what happened in life was just a matter of luck, good or bad. But he spent much of his time thanking some higher power for letting this miracle of new life happen for Emily and him. And for making the dream he had just about given up on come true.

Near the end of her second month, Emily woke up early, went into the bathroom, and moments later, started screaming. Joel jumped out of bed and rushed into the bathroom to find her standing in a pool of blood.

"I lost her," sobbed Emily.

Joel couldn't speak. Instead, he got busy, grabbed a few bath towels and stuffed them between Emily's legs to catch any more blood that might flow. While Emily cried, he helped her off with her nightgown and put her bathrobe around her. Then he walked her into the bedroom and sat her on the bed while he called the clinic.

The service answered. Joel said his wife seemed to be having a miscarriage. After a few moments, he heard the sleepy voice of Dr. Lane.

"This is Joel Sachs, Dr. Lane. Emily is bleeding profusely."

The doctor told him to get her to New York Hospital, and he would meet them in the maternity wing.

Joel helped Emily off the bed, out of the apartment, and into a taxi.

"Why is this happening, Joel? Why are we being punished?"

"I don't know, my darling," he said. "I don't know."

The hospital admitted Emily. Dr. Lane performed the necessary surgery to scrape her uterus.

When Emily awakened, Joel was by her side. He smiled at her.

"Hi," he said.

"Is it over?"

"Yes," said Joel.

"Was it a Molly or Max?

"He didn't say. All he said was you'll be fine."

"Fine?" she asked. "Did he really say I'll be fine?"

"He said we should definitely continue fertility treatments."

"I don't know," said Emily.

"He said you conceived once, so there's a good possibility you'll go all the way next time."

*　　*　　*

After a few weeks, Emily reluctantly agreed to give it three more months. "If after that I'm not pregnant," she said, "then I'm calling it quits."

"Okay," said Joel.

When the three months were over and Emily was not pregnant, she and Joel decided, with Dr. Lane's encouragement, to extend the effort—and their despair—for six more months. Beside the emotional cost, at the end of the six months they would have spent over $40,000, which was almost all their savings.

Two weeks after Emily's final insemination, she got her period. When she came out of the bathroom, she found a hammer in their tool box, went into the baby's room and began to destroy all the beautiful furniture, piece by piece. Joel stood at the entryway to the room and watched her in silence. She removed the layette from the white dresser, handed it to Joel and instructed him get rid of it. He went to the incinerator in the basement of their building and threw it in.

When he returned, the baby's room was a mass of wood slats and splints, yellows and whites.

They studied the room for a few minutes then went into their bedroom, got into bed, and lay there in sad silence until they fell asleep.

Fanny

Soon after her sixty-eighth birthday, Joel's older sister Fanny lay dying in a Florida hospice. It shocked him to realize that his flesh-and-blood sibling, the first born in the family, had refused to see or speak to him or Gloria, their younger sister, for over twenty years. He could never understand why Fanny, had made such a decision.

True, she had always had issues with Joel. For one thing, he had always been Rose's favored child, perhaps because he was the only son, which was often the case in Jewish families. Or perhaps it was because Rose didn't like her daughter's bitchiness any more than anyone else did. Fanny often complained that she was the unloved child in the family, an outsider. Joel would suggest to her that maybe if she altered her personality she'd be more loved, but that only served to intensify her hostility. She told him more than once to go screw himself. But she didn't stop talking to him.

Joel was a good student, hard working, and well liked. That was not true of Fanny. She was lazy, rude to her teachers, and threatening to her classmates. As a result, no one liked her. When Joel pointed this out, she would say that even if she had Joel's virtues, even if she worked hard and was nice and cooperative, she'd never be appreciated the way he was—and maybe she was right. She was deeply jealous of the approval he received. Still, she didn't cut him off until much later.

Harvey, her husband, turned against Joel from the moment he and Fanny started dating. He was a fount of hostile feelings and never at a loss to find cruel things to call Joel: "shithead", "asshole", "*Miss* Intellectual Prick", "*Miss* Four-eyed Fartface." Joel warned him to stop calling him names, but Harvey laughed and called him "sensitive sissy" or "flabby fairy." When Harvey started calling Gloria, the sister Joel adored, "fatty" and "pimple-face," making her cry, Joel told him, "You can call me anything you want, but Gloria is off limits."

"Or what?" asked Harvey.

"Or I'll get even," said Joel.

Harvey laughed at him, calling him "protector faggot" or "brother homo."

Joel asked Fanny to do something to put an end to her boyfriend's (and later husband's) insults, but she only scoffed and said, "What's wrong, sissy boy, is he hurting your feelings?"

Joel loathed them both, and he would leave any gathering the minute they appeared. Harvey would often call out something like, "Aw, is the little girl upset?"

Once, Rose heard Harvey call Joel "fag." White with rage, she rushed at Harvey, who was sitting on her sofa with Fanny. They were both eating ice cream, her right leg across his left thigh. Rose grabbed the bowl of ice cream away from him and growled, "What did you call my son?"

Harvey was thrown. He turned to Joel and said, "The little faggot needs his mama to protect him, huh?"

"Stand up," Rose commanded. Harvey obeyed. He was about two feet taller than Rose, but that didn't stop her. With her free hand she slapped him hard across the face and said, "Don't you ever call this boy names again, or I won't let you into my home."

Then she turned to Fanny. "You too," she told her daughter,

snatching her bowl away and handing it to Joel.

"Me?" asked Fanny, standing up. "What did *I* do?"

Rose slapped her hard and said, "You tell your husband he's not allowed to call your brother names, or I won't let you in here either, you hear me?"

"I can't tell my husband what to do."

"You better," said Rose, carrying their bowls of unfinished ice cream into the kitchen and dumping them into the sink.

But even that incident, infuriating as it was to Fanny, was not the one that led her to stop talking to Joel. Which is not to suggest that she was nice to him, but she didn't yet give him the silent treatment. Angry as she felt, she still acknowledged him when they were together and occasionally called him up to chat.

Years earlier, Joel had seen his mother sitting on a bench in Central Park with another man, kissing him passionately. Afterwards, deeply upset, Joel met Fanny at the Carnegie Deli, where they regularly had brunch together on Sundays. Fanny recognized that Joel was troubled by something, but he refused to tell her what it was. He implied that he didn't trust her, which insulted her, and she walked out of the restaurant, leaving him alone. Still, she continued talking to him and even continued to have Sunday brunch with him.

The event that did end their relationship made the least sense to Joel. But obviously it was significant to Fanny, more so than any of their earlier conflicts. Fanny and Harvey had moved with their children to a tract home in New Jersey, about two hours from Manhattan. One day Fanny called Joel to say that he and his wife had never visited her or her children in the two years since they'd moved to their new home.

"You call that a brother?" she asked him.

Although Joel could not find any great enthusiasm to visit, he agreed because he loved Fanny and Harvey's children, and they

loved him. He had babysat them. He had taken them on out-
ings to the theater, to museums, and to the circus when they
lived in New York. And despite all her cruelties to him, Joel
still felt a bond with his older sister. He had shared so much
of his young life with her, including the disharmony in their
family, the fights between their parents, and the birth of their
sister Gloria. Not least, Fanny had taught him ballroom dancing. She was a good dancer, and her instruction had turned
him into a good dancer.

Joel convinced a reluctant Emily—he had to beg her—to
come with him to visit Fanny and Harvey. He called Fanny
back and told her they would take the bus out and spend the
following Saturday there. But on Saturday morning, Joel awakened with a stabbing pain in his lower back. At the emergency
room of New York Hospital, he learned that he had a kidney
stone and that the intense pain— comparable, the nurse said,
to labor pains—would last until the stone passed. A bus ride to
New Jersey was out of the question. He couldn't possibly travel
for two hours and then be a congenial visitor, even on painkill-
ers. He called Fanny and explained.

Her response shocked him. "You're full of it," she said.

"You really think I'm lying, Fanny?"

"If you don't show up here today, Joel Sachs," she said in a
voice like steel, "I will never talk to you again. You can forget
about having an older sister for the rest of your life."

"Can't we make it next week if the stone passes?" Joel asked.

"It's today or never," said Fanny.

"You're being irrational."

Fanny hung up without replying.

Her threat upset him, but he was in too much distress to
argue with her. Emily took the phone, called Fanny back, and
confirmed Joel's condition.

"Mind your own business, Emily," Fanny said. "You're only an in-law." She slammed the phone down.

It took about six days, living on pain medication and drinking quarts of water, to flush out the stone. When it finally passed, Joel phoned Fanny to tell her the good news and offered to drive out the next Saturday. He was certain that by now she would be filled with regret over calling him a liar and hanging up on him the week before. But he was wrong. She was ice.

"I thought I made it clear that I'm through with you?"

"For God's sake, Fanny," he said. "I've been pacing around the apartment for six days and nights in the most intense pain I've ever known."

"Goodbye," she said and hung up.

Joel learned later that Fanny immediately had phoned Gloria to tell her that she was through with Joel.

"But he really did have a kidney stone," Gloria had said.

"If you defend him, I'm through with you, too."

"Joel's not a liar, and you know it."

"Don't call me again," Fanny had shouted. "Ever. You're on my shit list along with him."

And that was the end of their sisterhood.

Fanny had admitted to Joel once that he was one of the only people in the world she trusted and even "liked," yet now their relationship was over for a reason that made no sense. He regretted that he would no longer get to see her children. But at the same time, he was relieved to have Harvey out of his life.

Rose refused to believe that the separation was serious, let alone permanent. She kept urging Joel—daily at first, then weekly, and finally just once in a while—to "make up with your sister. It's a terrible thing for a brother and sister to be enemies." But Joel refused to initiate a reconciliation. He told his mother, "*I* didn't stop speaking to *her, she* stopped speaking to *me*. It's up to her to offer a truce."

Gloria wouldn't seek a rapprochement with Fanny either, for the same reason, and told Rose so.

Rose also badgered Fanny to make up with her siblings. But Fanny told her mother, "This is none of your business. I have no intention of ever speaking again to either of them." Rose argued with her for several months, but Fanny would not cave. It upset Rose when she invited all her children to dinner, and Fanny and Harvey refused to come because Gloria and Joel were going to be there. Rose expressed resentment over what they were all doing to her and promised to die of heartbreak because of it. But after a time she resigned herself to the reality that her children were never going to get back together. As it happened, Rose did die six months later—not from "heartbreak," but a heart attack.

Now, when Joel heard that Fanny had been diagnosed with ovarian cancer and was on her death bed, he felt real sadness to think that she could die totally estranged from him. He had hoped since the break-up that something would occur to reunite them: Fanny would come to her senses, Harvey would die, or their children would miss Uncle Joel and Aunt Emily and demand that Fanny make up with them. But nothing like that happened.

The news of Fanny's cancer had less of an effect on Gloria. From the day Lou had appeared at their school to inform Fanny and Joel that they had a new sister, Fanny never disguised her hatred of Gloria. Besides being favored by Lou and Joel, Gloria was prettier and more popular and smarter than Fanny. She never said a kind word to her younger sister. She never wanted to be with her. She never gave her a gift. She never praised her. She mocked her for being "an accident." Gloria couldn't recall if Fanny had ever kissed her. All she remembered was anger and jealousy and cruelty, sibling rivalry at its darkest and deepest.

In light of this history, Gloria felt nothing in reaction to the news of Fanny's illness. Fanny was just a memory, and not a happy one.

One night soon after Joel learned that Fanny was dying, he had a nightmare. In it Rose was still alive, and she was crying, "Oh, my Fanny, my Fanny! I'm losing my first-born child. There's nothing worse than outliving your own child. God in heaven, why couldn't it be me you cursed with cancer?"

Joel turned to Rose and said, "You're full of it, Ma. You don't *really* wish it were you with cancer. You've said yourself more than once that Fanny is a mean bitch."

Rose looked at him with a hideous scowl and said, "I love my Fanny with my whole heart, and my Fanny loves me. It may not look that way to some, but a mother and a daughter love each other even when they don't."

Joel responded to his mother's hypocrisy, "I, for one, am not going to pretend I feel sad about Fanny, because I don't, and I certainly don't wish I was the sick one and not her." He waved goodbye to an imaginary Fanny and called out, "Rot in hell!"

Rose glared at him and shouted, "You love her, don't tell me otherwise. Nobody likes her, but love is different than like, and you love her, and she loves you. You know I'm right."

The nightmare haunted Joel. A month later, Harvey phoned and begged Joel to come to the hospice in Florida to see Fanny before it was too late. Harvey told him that Fanny was delirious, but in her delirium she'd been calling Joel's name. "She's even calling *me* Joel," he said.

Joel said, "She hasn't talked to me for twenty years, Harvey. How can you expect me to travel down to Florida to say good-bye to her?

Harvey said that, in her delusional conversations, "she keeps repeating over and over that she was always unloved and she wants you to tell her you love her before she dies. She cries and cries until she falls asleep." Joel was silent for a moment, and Harvey added, "I know what she feels because my family never loved me, either. So please get here, Joel, before she passes."

Hearing this shook Joel and rekindled something that he thought had died. He suggested to Gloria that they go see Fanny for the last time.

Gloria was surprised and puzzled. "Why *me*? Harvey didn't say she asked for *me*. Just *you*."

"She's *our* sister, Gloria. We need closure."

"Not me. She was never a sister to me. She never treated me like a sister. She never showed me kindness or compassion or any humanity."

"There were moments between us, Gloria," said Joel, "when I really felt something for her. When we danced together. When we had brunches together and she confided things to me about her life. Her sadness. Her emptiness."

"That was *you*," said Gloria. "*I* never shared anything like that with her. She's been dead to me for years."

Joel told Gloria about his dream. "I know Mommy was telling me to go and see her."

"It was *your* dream, not *mine*."

"I need you to come with me, Gloria."

"She hated me, Joel. And I hated her."

"Please. I need you with me."

"Why?

"I just do."

Two days later, Joel and Gloria flew to Miami, checked into a motel, and took a taxi to the hospice where Fanny was approaching death.

On the way there, Joel tried to hide the anxiety he felt at the thought of seeing his alienated sister and her repulsive husband. But he couldn't keep it secret from Gloria. She knew him too well and patted his hand to calm him.

After a moment's reflection, he smiled. "Wouldn't it be amazing if we found a different Fanny? A Fanny who's warm and tender, sorry for her past behavior towards us, genuinely happy to see us? A Fanny whose heart is suddenly full of love?"

Gloria laughed. "Aren't fantasies fun?"

"Don't you think change is possible?"

"Not in Fanny's case."

"I'm trying to be optimistic," said Joel.

"That's fine," said Gloria. "But optimistic and unrealistic are two different things."

They reached the hospice, Joel paid the driver, and they started for the entrance. Joel stopped short and stared at Gloria.

"Should we or shouldn't we?" he asked.

"Let's get it over with," said Gloria, and led the way in.

Harvey, in a sweat suit, was dozing on a recliner in Fanny's room. It was bright and cheerful with sunlight pouring through the large window and, outside, a view of lush trees and clear blue sky. It was an ironic contrast to the dark reality of imminent death.

Fanny lay in bed, her face drawn and pale, and her hair white after having been dyed red or blond from the day she first saw a gray hair. Her skin was dry, her face a mass of wrinkles in every direction. Her eyes were wide open, her eyeballs glazed over and unfocused, and her mouth dripped drool. Joel and Gloria tried to hide their shock.

Harvey awakened with a start. "Oh, you made it," he said. "Good." He stood up. "Thanks for coming."

Joel nodded. Harvey extended his hand. Joel shook it.

Gloria didn't bother to greet him. Harvey didn't offer her his hand.

For the first time since Joel had known him, Harvey looked vulnerable, tearful, and very tired.

"She hasn't got long," Harvey said.

"Can she hear us?" asked Joel.

"Who knows?" replied Harvey. "Sometimes she answers when I talk to her, mostly she doesn't." He bent over Fanny and said quietly, "Your brother and sister are here, Babe."

Fanny didn't respond.

Harvey turned to Joel. "Say something to her. You're the one she's been asking for, so you should do the talking."

So many years of not speaking, thought Joel, and now he was expected to start a conversation as Fanny lay dying, possibly unable to hear. He looked at Gloria for encouragement.

Gloria broke the ice. "Hi, Fanny," she said. "It's Gloria. Joel and I have come down to see you."

"Why?" asked Fanny.

The question threw Gloria. But before she could answer, Fanny said, "To see me die, huh? I bet that'll give you a good laugh."

"You're not dying," said Harvey. "Don't be ridiculous."

"Shut up, Harvey," said Fanny. "Nobody's talking to you."

"You know what, Fanny?" said Joel. "On the way down here, I was telling Gloria about when we were kids, and you taught me to dance. Remember what a great rumba we did together?"

Fanny mumbled something indistinguishable.

"What did she say?" Joel asked Harvey.

Harvey nudged him out of the way and leaned over again. "What did you say, Babe?"

Her voice weak, Fanny said, "I'm talking to Joel."

Harvey moved out of the way. Joel took his place.

"You were a lousy dancer," said Fanny.

"What?" asked Joel. "You used to say I was pretty good."

"You danced like a girl," said Fanny.

Harvey laughed. "She still has a sense of humor, huh?"

"You wiggled your hips just like a girl," Fanny said.

"Well, if I did, it was your fault. You were my teacher, said Joel.

"I remember we were doing a Lindy in that casino in the Catskills," Fanny said, "and people were laughing at you and saying you danced just like a girl."

"Is this why I came all the way down here? So you could be a bitch and hurt my feelings?"

"I used to think you were going to be queer when you grew up."

Again, Harvey laughed.

"You really thought that?" asked Joel.

"A lot of people did," said Fanny. "Some of my friends. Even Mommy thought so."

"What?" Joel couldn't suppress his outrage.

"A couple of times I heard her ask Daddy if they'd raised a fairy."

"Still the same Fanny," said Gloria. "Even on her death bed."

"Keep it up, Fanny, and I'll walk right out of here," said Joel.

"She's telling it like it is," said Harvey. "I always thought you were queer, too."

"Well, I always thought you were a dumb asshole, Harvey," said Joel, "and I still do".

It was Fanny's turn to laugh.

"That's funny?" asked Harvey. "Your brother calls me a dumb asshole, and that's funny to you?"

"He's right," said Fanny.

"And you're a stupid cunt!" said Harvey.

"Thanks a lot for begging me to come with you," Gloria told Joel.

"What is *she* doing here, anyway?" asked Fanny.

"I wanted her to come with me," said Joel. "I thought maybe you'd like to see her too."

"You were wrong," said Fanny.

"Believe me, Fanny, this is the last place I want to be," said Gloria, "and you're the last person I want to see. You were awful to me my whole life."

"I was awful to everyone. I'm a total bitch. I always was. Joel was Mommy's favorite, and you were Daddy's favorite, but I was nobody's favorite, and I hated you both."

"You once told me that you liked me," said Joel. "You didn't call it love, but you called it like."

"I never loved anyone," said Fanny. "I have no love in me. I don't even know what love is. You have to *be* loved to *know* love."

"Well," said Joel, "Mean as you were, there were actually times when I felt love for you."

"You were blind," said Fanny. "I always told you to take off the rose-colored glasses."

"You were probably right," said Joel.

"You shouldn't have come," said Fanny. "I didn't want to see you."

Harvey protested. "That's bullshit! All you did was talk about him. You kept calling me by his name."

Suddenly, Fanny began to cry. Deep sobs. She wailed.

"What is it, Babe?" asked Harvey. "What's wrong?"

"I hate my life! I want to die!"

"Don't, Babe," Harvey pleaded. "You're breaking my heart."

"What heart, you schmuck?" said Fanny. "You don't have a heart!"

"Aw, Fanny..." Harvey pleaded.

"Go away! All of you!" cried Fanny. "Let the bitch die in peace!"

Harvey, frightened, leaned over and touched her shoulder gently. "Take it easy, Babe. Take it easy. Please."

Fanny shrugged his hand off.

A nurse appeared. "What's going on here?" she asked.

"Get them out of here," Fanny pleaded. "They're suffocating me!"

The nurse looked at Gloria and Joel.

"We're going," said Joel.

"I think that's a good idea," said the nurse.

Gloria left the room first, without a parting word to Fanny.

Joel looked at Fanny. "You really want us to go?"

Weeping, Fanny answered, "I just want to die." She turned away and stared at the wall.

Joel started out of the room, following Gloria and followed by Harvey. He stopped for a moment and turned back to Fanny. "Pathetic," he said. "Dying as you lived."

Fanny was silent.

Joel left.

In the waiting room, the three of them stood there avoiding each other's gaze.

"Some going-away party!" said Harvey.

The nurse came out of Fanny's room and informed them that Fanny was gone.

For a moment, no one spoke. Then Joel said, "Amen," and without another word, he and Gloria walked away.

Gloria

G loria was sixty and living in the house she and her husband, Raymond, had bought in Chicago, when, one Saturday, she decided to impose some order on their cluttered basement. She began by organizing the dozen or so scattered cartons of family memorabilia that her mother, Rose, had asked her to store a few years before she died. Until now, Gloria had ignored the cartons and more or less forgot about them. Today, as she stacked them neatly, she became curious and opened some. In the first couple, she found family photos from the time Rose and Lou were young and presumably in love, as well as others of her siblings and relatives.

It startled her to realize, studying the photos, how little she looked like the rest of the family. She saw a slight resemblance between herself and her mother in their smile. She and Joel had similar lips, and Fanny's eyes were shaped exactly like her own—although Fanny's were brown, hers blue. But it troubled her that she had no features in common with Lou, her late father, whom she had adored. She stared for a long time at the photos of the two of them together, but she saw no resemblance. Realizing that she looked different from the Sachses was not as surprising or unsettling as certain *specific* dissimilarities between her and them. She alone had blue eyes and hair the color of burgundy wine. This wasn't the first time she'd noted them, but this time it struck her sharply.

Then she came upon a box marked "Joel's Schoolwork." It was filled with her brother's homework, exams, essays, and stories from his years in high school and college. Among the stories was one called "The Accident," a title that stopped her, calling to mind the years when Fanny would refer to her regularly as "the accident." She began to read, and sure enough, it concerned her pre-natal history. By the end of the first page she was in a state of shock.

Joel—known as "Jack" in the story—was the narrator. He told how he'd overheard Rose ("Rachel") informing Lou ("Leonard") that she was pregnant for the third time. Leonard accused her of cheating, calling her a betrayer and a whore. Rachel denied the accusation, but Leonard was adamant.

"Who's the father, Rachel? Tell the truth," Joel had written.

"You are, Leonard."

"I don't believe you."

"May I die on the spot if I'm lying."

"I want you to have an abortion."

They argued for a long time—unaware that eight-year-old Jack was hearing every word. Rachel insisted that abortion was against the law and sacrilegious, and that abortionists were butchers who charged a fortune. Leonard threatened that if she didn't get rid of the child, he would never love it or accept it as his own. He won the argument when he told Rachel that if she didn't have an abortion, he would leave her. According to the narrator, "With two children to raise already, Rachel couldn't afford to lose Leonard's financial support, limited though it was by his gambling."

At this point, Gloria could barely read on, it was so painful. As Joel wrote, "Rachel was too far gone to abort," which is why Gloria ("Jean") existed. There was also a comment by the narrator on the irony that Leonard's unwanted child would become the object of his greatest devotion, greater than anyone else in the family or, for that matter, in the world.

Gloria was shattered. She didn't know if Joel's story was fiction or fact. Gloria wanted to believe it was made up, because it would devastate her if it were true. At the age of sixty, she would be looking back on a life that had been one big lie: the Lou she'd adored had not fathered her and had instead wanted her destroyed, her mother had been an adulteress, and Joel, whom she worshipped and trusted more than anyone, had kept the truth from her all those years.

If Gloria had known earlier that her father was someone else, she would have done everything she could to find him, or at least find out who he was. Maybe he was rich. Maybe he was educated and cultured. That would explain why she was so different from her parents, so much smarter and more tasteful than both of them, smarter than Fanny and prettier. She wondered why any man of culture and education—and possibly wealth—would have been attracted enough to her conventional, overweight, uncultivated mother to want to make love to her. Was it a one-time thing or had the affair continued for months or even years?

On the other hand, she told herself, "The Accident" could be fiction, invented by Joel as an assignment for a writing course. In fact, his teacher had given the story an "A" and commented, "This is a fascinating and provocative story. Well done."

"Oh, please," Gloria prayed aloud, "let it be make believe," aware as she did so that she was wasting her time. As an atheist, she didn't believe in prayer. In deep turmoil, she told Raymond what she had just read.

"You're sixty years old," he said. "Your mother's dead, your father's dead, your older sister's dead, all your aunts are dead, your whole family is dead except for you and Joel. How are you ever going to find out if your real father was someone other than Lou?"

"I don't know," said Gloria, "but I have to try."

"Why?" asked Raymond. "Why do you care so much?"

"It's about my *identity*. It's important to me."

"At *sixty*?"

"Age isn't the issue. Wouldn't you want to know the truth if you found out *your* father wasn't who you thought he was?"

"Personally," said Raymond, "I don't buy that Lou wasn't your real father."

"Well, it doesn't matter if *you* buy it or not—this is *my* problem. The first thing I'm going find out is if Joel and I have the same father."

"How?"

"DNA," said Gloria.

She went to the phone and called Joel in New York. Gloria asked him to meet her for a DNA test as soon as possible, to find out if they had the same father.

Joel was thrown into a state of anxiety. "What are you talking about?"

"I have to know once and for all who I am," said Gloria.

"What's this about, Gloria?"

"I have to know who my father is."

"Your father is Lou Sachs, *the man who raised you*," said Joel.

"There's more to it than that," said Gloria. "Genes. Identity—physical, emotional, psychological, spiritual—and my medical history. When I fill out forms for doctors, I always put down that my father had diabetes. But if Lou wasn't my father, I'm giving an *in*accurate history, and that's serious. I *have to* know who produced me."

"What makes you think you had a different father?"

"You know damn well what makes me think so."

"I do?"

"*Your story!*"

"What story?"

"*The Accident.*"

There was silence at the other end.

"Joel, please, please, please don't play games with me! You wrote it in college. It was among the stuff Mommy sent me when Raymond and I bought this house. I found it in one of the cartons."

"Something I wrote for school?"

"Yes. I always thought my being an accident meant I wasn't planned for. I had no idea it meant I was created by some stranger!"

"It was *fiction*, Gloria."

"Maybe it was, maybe it wasn't," said Gloria. "That's what I want to find out."

"You had no right to read something of mine without my permission."

"If it was fiction, what difference does it make?"

Joel was again silent.

"Mommy was a cheater, after all, wasn't she?" asked Gloria.

"I don't know," said Joel.

"That's why Daddy wanted her to get rid of me, right?"

"I don't know."

"You *do* know! Be honest with me, damn it!"

"It was just a story. For a creative writing class."

"Are you going to agree to a DNA test or not?"

"What if you find out that you did have a different biological father? Then what?"

"I'll let you know when I find out."

Sitting at his desk, Joel wondered what it would do to Gloria if she learned that Lou was not her father. That Rose was a cheater. That Joel and Gloria were just half-siblings. How would it affect their relationship? Would it change? If so, how? Half-sister or whole, Gloria was deep in his heart. But how could he turn her down? He told her he'd go through with the DNA test. It was agreed that she would send for a DNA kit, and she and Raymond would come to New York as soon as she had it. They would stay with Joel and Emily until the results arrived. That way, they'd all be together for the news, whatever it turned out to be.

Once Joel agreed to the test, Gloria wasted no time sending her order and a check for $300 to a lab at the University of Arizona. As she did so, she suffered from the thought that she might have had a father she would never know.

In New York, Joel was a wreck—guilty, anxious, and confused—while he waited for Gloria's call to tell him that the test kit had arrived and she and Raymond were on their way. He couldn't imagine the consequences for his beloved sister if and when she found out that his father was not her father.

Gloria hardly slept. At one point she called Joel from Chicago. "Maybe it will turn out that Lou was *my* father but not *yours*."

"I hope so."

"Are you serious?"

"Totally. Let's face it, Gloria, I never loved him."

"Well, *I* did!" said Gloria, hanging up disappointed.

Soon she phoned Joel again. "I'm sorry for being a pain, but if he wasn't your father, wouldn't you want to know who your real father is?"

"I'm too old to care."

"Do you think Mommy knew I wasn't Daddy's and kept it a secret all her life?"

"I guess it's possible."

"Maybe I never really knew her," said Gloria.

"You can't really know a person until you know her secrets," said Joel. "A lot of people take their secrets with them to the grave."

"I'm so depressed," sighed Gloria. "I feel like the ground has disappeared from beneath my feet."

"If I believed in God," said Joel, "I'd curse him for letting me write that fucking story."

Life went on as normally as possible in the days that followed. Both Joel and Gloria spent their time doing what they usually did—working—but there wasn't a moment when they weren't worrying about the upcoming test. On certain days, Gloria would find herself staring in a full-length mirror, trying desperately to find traces of Lou. She studied her hands, her feet, and her gestures in the hope that something would remind her of him. But nothing did.

She spent restless nights imagining all sorts of uncomfortable things. What if her real father wasn't Jewish and she was only *half* Jewish? If that were so and she had known, how would it have affected her life? She couldn't imagine being anything but totally Jewish. Not that she was religious. She didn't even believe in religion. She considered it something that divided people. But it disturbed her nevertheless to imagine Rose in bed with a man who wasn't a Jew. *Uncircumcised. Unkosher.*

After a few more days, the kit arrived, and Gloria trembled as she opened it and read the instructions. Then she phoned Joel.

"Is Tuesday all right for us to come?" she asked. "As soon as we have the specimens, we're supposed to put them in the envelope provided and send them off."

"You're sure you want to go through with this?" asked Joel.

"Absolutely," said Gloria. She hung up, still trembling.

On Tuesday, Gloria and Raymond arrived at JFK. Joel picked them up at the American Airlines Terminal and drove them to his apartment on West End Avenue. Joel and Gloria were more anxious than excited to see each other. Raymond, aware of their discomfort, tried to calm them down with stories about the flight from Chicago. He rattled on about a woman who was so frightened of flying that while the plane was taxiing, she turned to the passengers around her and prepared them for the possibility that she might become hysterical at take-off, perhaps screaming or even fainting in her seat.

"I'm okay once we're in the air," she promised, "but leaving the ground and landing freaks me out. You don't have to do anything. Don't try to help me. I get over it eventually. I'm just apologizing in advance."

Raymond's story didn't succeed in calming anyone. Quite the opposite.

"I know exactly what she was feeling," said Gloria. "I'm feeling the same thing myself right now."

Raymond suggested that they stop for lunch on the way to the apartment.

"No," said Gloria. "I want us to do the test first. Let's get it over with."

"What's the rush? I'm starving. She wouldn't let me eat the airplane food," Raymond complained to Joel.

"Every time he eats on a plane, he gets off feeling sick," said Gloria.

"The point is, I'm hungry," said Raymond.

"I'm hungry too," said Gloria, "but we came with a specific purpose. Afterward, we can all go to a nice restaurant and relax."

"You really think you're going to be able to relax while you wait for the lab report?"

"Look, Raymond, I started this whole thing and I paid for the kit and the airline tickets, which makes me the leader, so I should be the one to make certain decisions for the group—like when we eat and when we do the test. My decision is we do the test."

That ended the argument.

They reached the apartment. Emily met them at the door and greeted Gloria and Raymond with hugs and kisses. Emily and Gloria regarded each other as sisters, not in-laws. Emily suggested a shower or a nap so they could relax after the flight.

"First things first," said Gloria.

From her tote bag, she took the kit she'd received from the University of Arizona. Like a schoolteacher, and not the powerful attorney she was, Gloria read the instructions slowly and clearly. The only restriction: no coffee or tea four hours in advance of the test. Neither Gloria nor Joel had had anything to eat or drink—except water—since early that morning, six hours ago.

"The first thing Joel and I have to do is rinse our mouths three times with warm water," directed Gloria, reading from the instructions.

"Why *three* times?" asked Joel.

"It doesn't say why," she said.

She then explained about the cotton swabs resembling long Q-tips. "You and I each get two swabs," she told Joel.

"Whatever we do, we mustn't touch the cotton end with our fingers. We both swab the inside of our cheeks on both of the Q-tips, thirty swabs each cheek."

"Why *thirty*?" Joel asked.

"Because that's what it says," said Gloria. "Now, please stop with the 'whys.' Just do as it says. After we swab thirty times, the swabs have to dry for fifteen minutes. Then we can pack them according to the instructions and send them to the lab Fed-Ex. In a week or so, they'll call with the results."

"Before we start," said Joel, "I want a hug and kiss." He embraced Gloria and kissed her and told her that no matter what happened he loved her and hoped she'd feel the same way. Then he hugged Raymond. "That goes for you too."

"I'm not sure if you're my whole brother-in-law or my half brother-in-law," said Raymond, "but frankly, my dear, I don't give a damn."

"Don't kid around, Raymond," Gloria said. "I have no sense of humor about this."

Gloria and Joel went into the kitchen, filled two glasses with warm water, and rinsed. Then they went back into the living room, where Emily and Raymond were sitting, waiting for the big moment.

Gloria handed Joel two swabs and kept the other two.

"The instructions say that one of us should swab after the other, not both at the same time," she said. "Please don't ask me why."

Joel swabbed his mouth first as Emily counted to thirty. But somewhere around thirteen, Gloria started to giggle, which surprised Raymond, and he asked her what was funny. She didn't know, but she couldn't stop laughing. By then Joel found her giggles contagious, and although he tried to restrain himself, he started laughing so hard that he found it difficult to continue.

"You just got through saying you had no sense of humor about this," said Raymond.

"I know," said, Gloria, "but I can't help myself."

Emily and Raymond looked at them and at each other as if to corroborate that their spouses were behaving oddly.

Gloria kept trying to stop laughing, but that only made her hiccup, which made Joel laugh even harder. Gloria realized what she was causing, so she ran to the bathroom, during which time Joel managed to calm down and finish with both swabs.

"Maybe it's nerves," Raymond said.

Gloria appeared from the bathroom, now sober. But the minute she started swabbing, she giggled again, and that set Joel off again. Soon they were both hysterical. But even in her hysteria, Gloria managed to swab as Raymond counted to thirty. When she was done, the relief for all of them was tremendous.

Gloria rested the wet swabs against a cardboard provided by the lab. All four sat in silence as they waited for the swabs to dry, until Joel remarked, "Isn't it weird that your father's identity is in your saliva?" Which struck Emily and Raymond as hilarious, and they roared with laughter,

"It wasn't that funny," said Gloria.

After fifteen minutes, she carefully packaged the dry swabs, and the four of them walked to the Fed-Ex office on Broadway. Gloria sent the samples off, and Emily suggested they celebrate by going to a seafood restaurant up the block for champagne and lobster.

At the restaurant, influenced by the champagne and a suggestion by Raymond that Gloria's father might have been Marlon Brando or maybe, if he was Jewish, George Burns or Groucho Marx, all four of them screamed with laughter yet again and drew a good deal of attention to themselves.

"Given that Rose was a Democrat," said Emily, "maybe Gloria's father was one of the Kennedy brothers. After all, they were all famous womanizers."

By the time they got back to the apartment, Gloria was exhausted from the flight, her anxiety, the test, the laughing, the champagne, and the overeating. She plopped down on the living room sofa and, without warning, began to cry.

"What if Daddy wasn't my father?" she wailed.

Patiently, Joel reassured her, "No matter what the DNA tells us, sweetie, he *was* your father. Psychologically."

"Of course," said Emily.

"I told her that," said Raymond.

"So did I," said Joel.

"I loved him so," cried Gloria.

"And he loved you," said Joel. "And I've always loved you. I'll still be your brother and he'll still be your father, even from the grave, no matter what."

But Gloria couldn't be consoled. "I think we have to go home, Raymond."

"Home?" said Emily. "You just got here."

"I know," cried Gloria, "but I can't spend the next week with all of us waiting for the results. It's too emotional and nerve-wracking. I'll go crazy."

"We could go to a hotel," said Raymond. "We could treat this like a vacation."

"I want to go back to Chicago. I want to be in my own home, where I feel safe."

The rest of them looked at each other and shrugged.

"Okay," Raymond said, "I'll see if I can book us on a flight out today."

Gloria apologized over and over again. "But I can't help myself. The stress is too much."

At 5:30, Emily and Joel drove Gloria and Raymond back to the airport, dropped them off at the terminal, kissed them goodbye, and watched them disappear inside. Gloria was still weeping when she called back to Joel and Emily as she entered, "I'll phone you as soon as I hear anything."

Gloria and Joel spoke on the phone frequently over the next several days. Each time, she swore she was fine, and each time it was obvious that she was not. Luckily, she had her work to distract her. The one time Raymond answered the phone, he admitted to Joel that Gloria was a wreck, she regretted ever having insisted on the DNA test, and, for the first time in their marriage, he was finding it difficult to live with her.

As for Joel, pretty sure of what the outcome would be, he was weak with worry about Gloria, certain that she wouldn't handle it well. In order to get through the week without falling apart, he did everything possible to force the matter from his mind. Sometimes he was successful, especially when he was teaching and totally absorbed in the work. But for a few nights, after speaking on the phone to Gloria, he had a rough time sleeping, and he surprised himself by taking tranquilizers to help him.

The following Tuesday, at about 5 P.M., Gloria called.

"We have different fathers," she said by way of a greeting. Her voice had no affect.

Joel was silent, not really surprised, although his heart sank.

"I guess that means she was a whore," Gloria continued.

Joel didn't know what to say, so he said nothing.

"And what does it say about Daddy? If Mommy was a whore,

then Daddy was a cuckold."

"I guess," said Joel.

"How can you be so cool about it? Doesn't it upset you?"

"Of course it does. I'm upset for *you*."

"I'm just your half-sister now."

"Gloria, believe me, I feel no different about you today than I've ever felt."

"Well, it helps to know that."

There followed a long silence.

"Are you all right?" Joel asked.

"No," said Gloria. "My whole life is in ruins."

"I think you're making too much of it."

"Raymond thinks so, too."

"Where *is* Raymond?"

"He's standing right here next to me, rubbing my back."

"How can I help you feel better?"

"You can't."

Another long silence followed. Then Gloria said, "I'll never know whose genes I have."

"Well, we know a lot of them are Mommy's."

"That's not comforting."

Joel had the impulse to laugh, but he didn't.

Gloria said, "You know what really bothers me?"

"What?"

"I'll never be able to stop thinking about this for the rest of my life."

Joel was silent once more. He realized that was true, and he felt terrible.

After a few moments of silence, Gloria said, "I'll let you go."

"Gloria…" Joel said.

She cut him off. "I can't talk anymore."

They hung up.

*   *   *

For a while, Gloria became obsessed with finding out who her real father was. She called a few surviving relatives who lived around the country and were old enough to possibly have some information.

She called a third cousin, Andrew Liebowitz, who lived in Toronto and was her age. As children living in the Bronx, they had been very close. After Andrew's initial surprise at hearing from Gloria after so many years, he asked, "Are you calling just to touch base or is there something specific you want to talk about?"

Gloria said, "Andrew, before your mother died, did she ever say anything as far as you know about my mother being a cheater?"

"Rose?" said Andrew. "A cheater?"

"This is very difficult for me," said Gloria, "but your mother was very close to my mother, and I wonder if my mother ever told her that Lou was not my father."

"Are you serious?"

"Please don't make this harder for me than it is, Andrew. I found out that I had a different father, but I don't know who he was, and I thought maybe…"

Andrew interrupted her. "I don't know anything about it, Gloria. You've taken me by complete surprise."

He suggested Gloria call another cousin, Manny Farkas, who might know something. Gloria asked Andrew not to say anything about this to anyone. "It's too humiliating."

Andrew said he understood what she was going through. "I'll never tell a soul, so help me God."

But Gloria knew he'd be on the phone the minute they hung up, spreading the word to everyone in the family who was still alive. She didn't much care. If her mother was a whore, she deserved to be the subject of gossip.

Gloria called Manny Farkas, but it turned out the Farkases never liked the Sachses and never socialized with them. Manny knew nothing about Rose's sex life, and sounded delighted to hear the scandalous news.

The few other relatives she called were all, like Andrew, shocked to learn that Rose had been a cheater, and that Gloria was not Lou's daughter. Most of them responded with some version of "We always thought Rose was such a nice person."

Soon after she'd made the calls, Gloria called Joel in New York, more frustrated and desperate than ever to know the truth. Joel finally revealed the secret he'd carried with him for over forty years. He told her about having seen their mother on a park bench "with a man whose hair was the exact color of yours, and I saw them kiss. At that point, I was worried she would see me, and I was too upset to watch any more, so I left."

"Oh, my God!" said Gloria, the atheist. "Oh, my God in heaven! That really happened?"

"I wish I'd never seen it."

"How come you never told me?"

"I didn't see any point. I thought you'd be better off not knowing anything about it."

"In other words, you've kept it from me all my life!'

"Yes," said Joel, guilt-ridden. "It never occurred to me that you'd find out about him."

"How could *you*, of all people, betray me like that? I'm a total mess about it. Didn't you realize that it would have been easier for me if I'd known sooner?"

"I just couldn't deal with it, honey. I thought it would devastate you. I knew how attached you were to Daddy. So I tucked it away in the back of my mind and tried not to think about it."

"You would have saved us the bother and anxiety of going through the DNA test."

"I feel like such a fool. I'm so sorry."

There was a long pause.

Then Joel said, "He was very handsome, Gloria. And he looked very intelligent."

"Really?"

"Yes."

Gloria was silent for a long while.

"You look a lot like him," said Joel.

Gloria said nothing.

"Are you okay?" asked Joel.

Gloria didn't answer.

Joel grew worried. "Gloria?"

Actually," she finally said, "I think I feel much better. Isn't that weird?"

"I love you," said Joel.

"I love you, too," said Gloria.

They never discussed it again.

Best Friends

J oel Sachs opened his email one morning and was surprised
to find a note from his best childhood friend, Izzy Peckman,
whom he hadn't seen for almost fifty years. According to Izzy,
a funny political cartoon had been forwarded to him online,
and Izzy happened to notice that among the recipients was
Joel Sachsaphone. He assumed correctly that "Sachsaphone"
must be Joel's online moniker so he decided to write in the
hope of reconnecting. Izzy, in his early seventies like Joel, was
living in Indianapolis, divorced for many years, and retired
from chemical research. He had three married children, one
of whom lived and worked in Zurich, and two who lived in the
Northwest. Izzy was going to be in New York the following
month to see a medical specialist "about some issues I've been
dealing with," and wondered if he and Joel could get together
for lunch or dinner or just coffee. Joel gave the matter some
thought and decided that it would be rude not to make himself
available. After all, they'd been best friends from the time Joel
was nine and Izzy ten, a friendship that lasted into their early
twenties. So Joel wrote back that he would be delighted, and
that Izzy should let him know when he'd be in the city and
where he'd be staying. Joel said he'd arrange a time and place
to meet for lunch and send Izzy the information.

As a kid, Izzy had lived in a tenement house, similar to
Joel's, on the corner of the same Bronx street. Izzy was not

good-looking. Joel remembered a face covered with acne. Not normal acne, but extra-large pimples, many of them blood red. Izzy picked at them or squeezed them unconsciously but incessantly—the way Joel bit his finger nails—until the pimples oozed pus or blood. An intellectual full of opinions about everything, he talked incessantly. More precisely, he croaked, and he clucked when he laughed. The other boys picked on him mercilessly for his pimples, for his croaking and clucking, and for his misfortune of having the last name Peckman. They called him "Pecker" or "Peckerhead" or "Pimpleface" or "Pickleman" or just "Pickle." Sometimes the name-calling made Izzy cry. Once, he and Arnie Geller got into a fistfight because Arnie called him "Peckerman the Pickle with a pecker that's *shtickle*." He was the butt of dozens of cruel jokes, including an occasional one made up by Joel himself, which hurt Izzy deeply:

"Heck, man,
There goes Peckman.
Someone told me
He eats *dreck*, man.
Poor Peckman,
Geh aveck, man."

The guys in the crowd applauded Joel's "poetry." Izzy looked at Joel with deep hurt. Joel hated himself for making jokes at Izzy's expense, and he promised himself each time he did it that he'd never do it again. In fact, Joel was devoted to Izzy, who was gentle, loyal, a fierce liberal, and full of compassion for every living thing—more than enough reason, as far as Joel was concerned, to love someone and treat him with respect. Joel always apologized to Izzy afterwards for his jokes, and Izzy always forgave him. Izzy was Joel's biggest supporter and defender. He told Joel more than once that with his personality and his brain, he would surely amount to something great. Hearing that from Izzy made Joel proud. And yet, Joel could not resist every now and then making jokes about Izzy to win the approval of the other boys.

Once each summer during their early teen years, Joel and Izzy would take the subway to Coney Island and spend the day there, eating three Nathan's hot dogs each with a side of french fries and a large Coke, and riding the Cyclone six times in a row. A sign warned anyone who wore glasses to leave them with the roller-coaster operator to avoid having them fly off during the ride. Izzy and Joel would always argue about whether or not to heed the warning. Joel would want to, but Izzy was strongly opposed because he was sure the operator would steal their glasses and sell them.

"Who's gonna buy somebody else's glasses?" Joel asked.

"Plenty of people," answered Izzy.

"But they're prescription glasses. Who has the same prescription as you or me?"

"They'll buy them for the frames," Izzy said.

Izzy always won the argument even though Joel thought it was ridiculous, and the boys would put their glasses into a pocket of their pants. The Cyclone was a rough ride full of twists and turns and sharp descents which provided its appeal, and inevitably each year, when the ride was over, both myopic boys' lenses were smashed, and they'd have to leave Coney Island and make their way to the subway and home half-blind. The worst part was telling their parents they'd broken their glasses and needed new ones. After three summers of this, their mothers prohibited them from going to Coney Island and coming home with broken glasses.

Sometimes on days when Joel would come to pick up Izzy to go to the movies, Joel would stand in the lobby of Izzy's building and call up the three stories, "Izzy! Hey, Izzy Peckman! Movie time!" More often, if there was enough time, he walked up the three flights and called for Izzy in the Peckman apartment. He loved seeing Mrs. Peckman, a short, chubby woman who was always working in the kitchen wearing an apron full of food stains. She spoke with a slight Russian accent. A lit cigarette always dangled from her lips, the smoke curling into her eyes, causing them to tear, sometimes choking her and causing a harsh smoker's cough. She teased Joel each time she saw him, calling him "homely thing," which Joel relished, knowing she meant it affectionately.

But Izzy didn't appreciate his mother's humor or irony. It annoyed and embarrassed him. "Ma-a-a!" he'd whine, "his name is *Joel*, not 'homely thing'!" To which Mrs. Peckman would respond, "Joel knows I'm only kidding." And Joel would confirm it. "It's true, Izzy. It doesn't hurt my feelings."

Izzy's father wasn't around except in the evenings, after work. The occasional times Mr. Peckman was home when Joel was there, he would say little. He'd be watching television news and talking back to the newscasters. "Eisenhower's an anti-Semite! Why don't you tell the truth for once!" Remarks like those and the fact that Izzy never left the house without kissing his father on the mouth were the only things Joel actually knew about Mr. Peckman. Joel had never kissed his father anywhere but on his cheek. And Lou Sachs had never put his lips anywhere near Joel's skin. Joel envied Izzy more for that shared intimacy with his father than for anything else about him.

When Joel and Izzy were together, there was a never-ending stream of conversation. They talked politics and news of the day and sports, especially baseball—or rather, Izzy did most of the talking because he knew more than Joel about most things. They talked about friends and teachers and school, and their plans and hopes for the future. Joel thought of Izzy as his mentor. Izzy read the newspaper every day, and, among other things, he quoted to Joel the injustices that were being done to Ethel and Julius Rosenberg. He knew the batting average of every Yankee player and the record of every Yankee pitcher, and he knew the names of every senator in Congress, junior and senior, as well as their voting records. Joel wasn't all that invested in politics except when he heard his father make some comment like "I hate both candidates. I'm not voting in this election." Then Joel would wonder why his father was so angry, and he would discuss it with Izzy, who would say, "Your father's probably a secret Fascist." Joel usually made a meager attempt to defend Lou: "How can a Jew be a Fascist?"

"You'd be surprised," Izzy would say mysteriously.

Privately, Joel had a pretty low opinion of his father, so although he defended him to Izzy, it actually gave him a charge to hear his father slurred.

Izzy couldn't believe that Joel knew nothing about baseball. Izzy not only knew all the Yankee statistics but went regularly to Yankee Stadium to watch the games. He also played stickball and softball and was famous on the block for his exceptional pitching.

"I can't believe you've *never* been to a baseball game!" Izzy would say over and over.

Joel was intimidated by the passion with which Izzy said this, but he always responded that he preferred to spend his money on tickets to a Broadway show. He'd buy the cheapest seat, usually in the last row of the second balcony. Where he sat didn't matter. Every show he saw excited him, if not for the play itself then for an acting performance or the set or the costumes. Seeing *Guys and Dolls*, his first theater experience, had been one of the most exciting events in his life and created in him a love for the theater that he would carry with him throughout his life.

But Izzy thought it was just as important for Joel to know something about baseball, so he insisted Joel memorize the batting averages of every Yankee player. Over and over, Izzy would repeat the numbers, changing them whenever a player's average changed. But Joel found it impossible to memorize numbers associated with a game that held no interest for him.

One day, however, Izzy insisted that Joel sacrifice going to the theater and come with him instead to a ball game. When he mentioned how fantastic the hot dogs at Yankee Stadium were, Joel agreed to go. He found himself having a nice time because of the hot dogs and peanuts and Cracker Jacks and because of Izzy's enthusiasm for the game. Izzy shouted both praise ("Way to go, Yogi!") and condemnation ("Replace the pitcher, he stinks!") at the top of his lungs. But at one point during the seventh-inning stretch, Joel asked Izzy if Yogi Berra and Larry Berra were related. Izzy threw up his hands in despair and said, "I give up. You're hopeless. Yogi Berra and Larry Berra are the same person!"

Eventually, Joel talked Izzy into coming with him to the theater to see *South Pacific*. Izzy resisted, but Joel reminded him that the musical had won the Pulitzer Prize, and if Joel had agreed to see a ball game then Izzy was obliged to return the favor. Izzy conceded, and it turned out that seeing great performers, Mary Martin and Ezio Pinza, in a great musical floored him. He was so moved that he couldn't speak after the curtain came down until they got outside. Then the show was all he could talk about.

"Prejudice!" exclaimed Izzy. "I never realized you could see plays about important issues like prejudice on Broadway. Especially a *musical!*"

From that point on, he was hooked on the theater and went with Joel whenever he could afford it. Theater tickets, even at only at $2.20, were considerably more expensive than bleacher seats at Yankee Stadium, which were only fifty cents, so it took both boys several weeks to save up enough for just one show—plus subway fare and an overpriced snack at intermission. Between plays, they would go back to Yankee Stadium for a double-header when the Yankees were playing at home.

One afternoon when Joel was eleven and Izzy twelve, Joel started up the stairs of Izzy's building, intending to pick Izzy up on the way to the movies and say hello to Mrs. Peckman. After walking up six steps, he noticed a pink wallet lying on the seventh step. His heart started racing as he imagined that the wallet contained a treasure—maybe a hundred dollars. It excited and frightened him. His body tensed up, and he found that it was actually painful to bend over and pick up the wallet because he was so rigid. He panicked. How could he leave the wallet behind for someone else to find? That would be insane. Suddenly, upstairs, he heard a door slam and a key lock it. Then he heard footsteps coming down the stairs. He realized that whoever was coming would probably have no trouble bending and taking the wallet, and he discovered then that he could bend over without difficulty and grab the wallet. He stuffed it into his jacket pocket and ran up the stairs.

When Izzy opened the door, Joel grunted, "I don't know what to do!"

"About what?" asked Iggy.

"This," said Joel, holding up the pink wallet.

"Come on in," Izzy whispered, to avoid being heard by his mother.

Mrs. Peckman called from the kitchen, "Who's there, Izzy?"

Izzy, with a slightly shaky voice, answered. "It's only Joel, Ma."

"That homely thing?" called his mother.

Izzy scowled. "She has one joke in her entire repertoire!" Of the wallet, he asked, "Where'd you get it?"

"I found it on the steps. It was just laying there."

"How much is in it?"

"I don't know. I'm too nervous to open it."

"Give it here," said Izzy, who took the wallet and investigated. He found a bill and held it up.

"Twenty!" said Izzy.

"Wow!" said Joel.

"And some keys."

Just then Mrs. Peckman entered and, exhaling cigarette smoke, scolded Joel. "You don't say hello to me anymore?"

"Oh, gee, Mrs. Peckman, I'm sorry. But something happened on the way up here…"

"Shush," Izzy told Joel.

"Why *shush*?" asked Mrs. Peckman.

"Nothing," replied Izzy. "It's between Joel and me."

"Is that money?" Mrs. Peckman asked, pointing to Izzy's hand.

Izzy tried to hide it behind his back.

"What's going on here?" Mrs. Peckman asked. A long ash from her cigarette fell to the floor. "Where'd you get that money?"

"I found this wallet on the way up," Joel blurted out. "The money was in it."

Mrs. Peckman was shocked. "Twenty dollars? What are you going to do with so much money?"

"He's not keeping it," said Izzy.

"I'm not?" asked Joel.

"It wouldn't be ethical. There are keys in it. One of them must be a mailbox key. We'll try all the mailboxes. If the owner lives in this building, the key will fit one. That will tell us who it belongs to, and we'll give it back."

"You're an honest boy, Izzila," said his mother. "You make me proud. I raised you well." She gave him a kiss. She gave Joel a kiss. And she went back to the kitchen.

"You're right, Izzy," said Joel, with mixed feelings. "I never would've thought of that."

"Let's go," said Izzy, and he led the way downstairs to the lobby, clutching the wallet with one hand and picking at a pimple with the other.

Joel followed like Dr. Watson trailing Sherlock Holmes, excited to be playing detective for a good cause. "Imagine how happy the person is going to be when we return the money," he said.

"It will teach the person that even capitalists can be moral," said Izzy.

He took the mailbox key off the ring in the wallet and started trying it in mailboxes. After a few failures, Joel asked, "What are we gonna do if it doesn't fit any? What if he lives somewhere else?"

"Who?" asked Izzy.

"The person who owns the wallet."

"It's probably a *she*, not a *he*. The wallet is pink."

"True," said Joel, embarrassed that he hadn't figured that out. "But then would it be ours?"

Izzy wasn't sure of the answer. But he was saved from having to provide one by the appearance of Mrs. Baum, who was coming out of the apartment closest to the bank of mailboxes.

"What are you kids doing?" she asked with suspicion.

"Oh, hi, Mrs. Baum. My friend Joel here found a wallet on the steps, and we're trying to find out who it belongs to," Izzy explained.

The face Mrs. Baum made indicated that she didn't believe him.

"Honestly, Mrs. Baum, there are keys in the wallet. So we're trying to find out if the mailbox key fits any of these mailboxes, and if it does..."

"Okay," she interrupted. "I believe you. I know your mother. She's a nice woman. If I find out you're lying, I'll tell her, and it will break her heart!"

"He's not lying," Joel said.

"I hope not."

When Mrs. Baum was gone, Izzy told Joel, "Some people think everyone's up to no good."

"Like my sister Fanny," said Joel.

"Here we go!" announced Izzy. "The key fits this one."

"It does?" asked Joel with a trace of disappointment.

Izzy read the name on the box. "Wortman," he said. "I never heard of a 'Wortman.' He must be new here."

"You mean *she*," Joel said.

"Maybe she's married," said Izzy, annoyed to be one-upped by Joel.

"Does it say her apartment number?".

"6E."

By the time they reached the sixth floor, they were out of breath—more from nerves than exertion. Izzy rang the bell. There was no response. He rang again. Still no response.

"What if nobody's there?" Joel asked.

"We'll try again later." He squeezed another pimple.

"You have blood on your face."

"Oh," said Izzy, taking his handkerchief from his back pocket and wiping off the blood. "Better?" he asked Joel.

"You should stop squeezing your pimples."

"I know. It's a bad habit."

"I have to stop biting my nails," said Joel. "It's *my* bad habit."

Suddenly, the door opened, startling Joel and Izzy. A man in pajamas, presumably Mr. Wortman, stood there, half asleep.

"Yeah?" he asked gruffly.

"Did you lose a wallet?"

"Not that I know of. It could be my wife's, though. Let me see it."

"First I need a description," said Izzy. "What color is your wife's wallet?"

"Pink," said Mr. Wortman. "I think."

"You 'think'?" said Izzy.

"It's pink," said Wortman, impatient to get back to sleep.

"Okay," said Izzy and handed Mr. Wortman the pink wallet.

"Yeah, that's hers," he said. "Thanks."

Izzy said, "She oughtta be more careful. There's twenty dollars in it and no ID."

"You're right," said Wortman. "If she hadda work nights like me to earn that twenty bucks, she'd be more careful. I'll talk to her about it."

The boys turned to go, pleased with themselves, although Joel was torn. It would have been great to be able to give his mother twenty dollars.

"Wait a minute," called Mr. Wortman. "I wanna give you something."

The boys stopped. "A reward?" asked Izzy.

"Right," said Wortman and disappeared inside.

The boys looked at each other.

"We're getting a reward?" asked Joel.

"You deserve one," said Izzy.

Joel said, "You mean 'we.'"

"No, Joel," said Izzy. "That's nice of you, but *you* found it, so the reward belongs to you."

"I found it, but *you* figured out how to find the owner," said Joel. "It belongs to *us*."

Mr. Wortman returned and handed each boy a coin.

"Thanks again," said Mr. Wortman, closed his door, and disappeared.

"A measly quarter," grumbled Izzy.

"Each," said Joel.

"Fifty measly cents," sneered Izzy.

"Well, it was nice of him to give us anything," said Joel.

"He should've given us at least a dollar each."

They started back down the stairs.

"So what are you gonna do with your money?" asked Joel.

"I don't know. I'll probably put it in the *pishka* for Israel at Hebrew school. What about you?"

"I'm giving mine to my mother. She really needs it."

"Oh, good idea," said Izzy. "Maybe I'll give mine to my mother, too. I'll tell her 'the homely thing' gave me the idea."

Joel's mother was ironing in the kitchen when he came home. The window was wide open because the apartment was hot, especially with the iron steaming. Rose was sweating and grouchy.

"Hi, Mommy," said Joel. "Guess what."

"I'm dying from this heat, that's what," whined Rose.

"Seriously, Ma, guess what."

"Where were you anyway? Why didn't you tell me where

214

you were going? You know I worry."

"I went over to Izzy's. We were gonna go to the movies. I told you that."

"Oh."

"So guess what, Ma."

"Oh, for God's sake, what?"

"I found a wallet."

Rose stopped ironing. "A wallet?" she asked.

"A pink one. With a twenty-dollar bill in it."

"*Twenty dollars?* Where is it?"

"Let me tell you what happened."

"Where's the twenty dollars?"

"It's a long story."

"I don't want stories. Where's the money?"

"Mommy, please let me tell you."

"You don't have it, do you?" said his mother, her throat tight, her voice dry.

"We found out who it belonged to, and we gave it back."

"What?"

"There was a mailbox key in it, so Izzy got the idea that we should try all the mailboxes and see if it fit one. And it did."

"You listened to *Izzy Peckman*?" said Rose.

"It was the right thing to do, Ma. Even Mrs. Peckman said so."

"Mrs. Peckman? Since when is Mrs. Peckman your mother?"

"She's not my mother, *you're* my mother," said Joel, "but Mrs. Peckman is a mother, too."

"Why didn't you come home and tell *me* about it? Do you have any idea how I could use that twenty dollars?"

"I know, Mommy, but it belongs to someone else. I'm sure the person can use it, too."

"I wish you'd stop being friends with Izzy Peckman," said

Rose, defeated. "He's a bad influence. And he's funny-looking—with the pimples all over him."

"We got a reward though, Mommy. We each got twenty-five cents."

Rose scowled. "A quarter?"

Handing the quarter to Rose, Joel said, "Here. It's for you."

Rose looked at Joel's open hand and the quarter lying on his palm, and she started to cry.

"What's wrong? Why're you crying?"

"Do me a favor, Joelly, go outside and play."

"Are you mad, Ma?"

"No. I just have to finish my ironing."

"Oh. Okay." He put the quarter on the end of the ironing board and started out. "Buy yourself something nice, Mommy."

"Okay," said Rose.

Joel could hear tears in Rose's voice. He assumed they were tears of happiness.

The following year, Joel saved up two dollars in an envelope marked "For Mother's Day" and bought his mother a corsage of three pink roses.

"Roses are my favorite flowers, Joelly, especially pink ones," she said.

"I know," said Joel, pleased. "That's why I got them for you."

"You're the sweetest son any mother could ever hope for. I'm putting the corsage in the refrigerator. That way, the roses will stay fresh."

Over the following week, Joel never saw his mother wear the corsage. He checked the refrigerator every day to make sure the roses were still alive. On the third day, he noticed they were starting to wilt. On the fourth day, the edges of the petals were turning brown. On the fifth day, the flowers were dead.

Heartbroken, he asked his mother why she hadn't worn the corsage. "Did you forget about it, Mommy? Did you forget it was in the refrigerator?"

"No, Darling," she replied, "I didn't forget. It's just that…" Rose paused. Her voice became a whisper. "I've had my period. When a woman has her period and she touches flowers, they die. So I'm sorry, Joelly, I couldn't wear the beautiful corsage. But I'll save it and dry the flowers. They'll still be beautiful."

Later that day, Joel and Izzy were in the schoolyard, playing slug against the brick wall. Izzy played with his usual intensity and determination. Joel, hardly focused, missed more balls than he hit. Izzy was annoyed and stopped the game. "What's with you, Sachs? You're playing like a girl."

Joel decided to tell Izzy the story of the corsage. He ended by saying, "So after five days it was still in the refrigerator but it was dead."

"How come she didn't wear it?" asked Izzy.

"She said it was because she had her period."

"Her what?"

"Her period."

"You mean like a dot that comes at the end of a sentence?"

"Not that kind of period," said Joel. "I'm talking about the kind that women have. Where they bleed."

"Bleed?" Izzy was startled and repulsed.

"Blood comes out of their vagina."

"Yuck!"

"Every woman has a period."

"*Every* woman?"

"Yes."

"Are you telling me that *my* mother has blood coming out of her vagina?"

"She's a woman, isn't she?" asked Joel.

"Of course."

"Then she has a period," said Joel, suddenly the teacher. "Once a month."

"You're nuts," said Izzy.

"Didn't you ever hear of Kotex?" Joel asked.

"I've seen it under the sink in the bathroom."

"Well, that's what your mother uses to absorb the blood when she has her period."

Izzy's eyes rolled. "You're making me a little nauseous, you know that?"

"Well, it's something you should know about."

Izzy thought hard for a few moments and then said to Joel, "Come on." He led Joel out of the schoolyard.

"Where are we going?" Joel asked.

"I have to get to the bottom of this."

After they walked in silence for two blocks, they came to Rubin's Pharmacy. Izzy led the way in.

"What are we doing *here*?" asked Joel.

"You'll find out."

The pharmacist, Mr. Rubin, was behind the counter filling a prescription. He stopped and asked, "Can I help you, boys?"

"I hope so," said Izzy. "Do you mind if I ask you a personal question?"

"Go right ahead," said Rubin.

"I hope it won't make you angry," said Izzy.

"Try me," said the pharmacist.

"Is it true that women get a period and blood comes out of their vaginas?" Izzy whispered.

Rubin cleared his throat and asked, "How do you know about such things at your age?"

"My mother told me about it," said Joel.

"Did she explain *why* women get their period?" asked Rubin.

"No," said Joel.

"It's nature's way of cleaning them out and preparing them to get pregnant. It's one of nature's miracles," said Mr. Rubin.

Izzy was flabbergasted. "Blood coming out of their hole is a miracle?" he asked.

Before Rubin could say more, Joel said, "My mother told me that she couldn't wear a corsage I gave her for Mother's Day because she had her period. She said when a woman has her period and touches flowers, the flowers die. Is that true?"

The pharmacist hesitated before answering. "Well, some women believe that. Some women think it's superstition and some women think it's real."

"What do *you* think, Mr. Rubin?" asked Joel.

"I think you should always believe what your mother tells you."

Joel was relieved. "I *do* believe her."

"Is there a lot of blood?" Izzy asked the pharmacist.

"Well," said Mr. Rubin, "some women bleed a lot, and some bleed a little."

"And you really think it's a miracle?"

"Yes, Izzy, I do," said Mr. Rubin. "The miracle of reproduction."

Joel and Izzy left. Joel felt good. Izzy was upset.

"I don't think Rubin knows what he's talking about. I wish I could ask my mother if she bleeds," he said.

"She does," said Joel. "Mr. Rubin wouldn't lie."

"I just wish I could ask her."

"Why don't you?"

"She'd wash my mouth out with soap. That's what she did once when I told her if she didn't make chocolate pudding she'd go to hell."

"Well, if you're not going to ask her, you'll just have to believe Mr. Rubin and me."

"Maybe I can find out something about it in the encyclopedia. Maybe I'll go to the library tomorrow and look it up."

"Good idea," said Joel.

They arrived back at the schoolyard and resumed the game of slug, both preoccupied with blood and vaginas.

One Saturday, Joel and Izzy and their friend Danny Farkas went to the Loew's Boulevard to see Greer Garson and Walter Pidgeon in *Mrs. Miniver*. The movie was considered a serious drama about the effects of World War II on a British family. But somehow it struck the three boys as funny, especially when Joel began to mimic Greer Garson's British accent. That started them giggling, then laughing. Soon all three of them were mimicking her every word until the audience, mainly adults, grew irritated and complained to the "matron"—as older female ushers were called—that the boys were disturbing them. The matron, a tough middle-aged woman in a white dress that resembled a nurse's uniform, shined her flashlight in their faces. "Get up and come with me," she ordered. They stopped fooling around and followed her into the manager's office, quaking with fear.

The manager was a big, overweight man. His suit was so tight that the fat of his belly and waist bulged over his belt and his shirt strained to stay closed. He was sitting behind a desk, playing with the nub of a pencil, when the matron led them in.

"These boys were causing a disturbance, Tiny."

When she called the manager "Tiny," Izzy started giggling. The manager turned red with rage.

"What the hell is so funny, pimple-face?"

Joel, scared out of his wits, elbowed Izzy to make him stop. But that made Izzy laugh more.

"I asked you something, four-eyes. What's funny?"

"I don't know," said Izzy and laughed even harder.

"Cut it out, Izzy," Danny muttered.

"I can't."

"You think I'm funny?" asked Tiny.

Izzy couldn't answer. He was laughing too hard.

"You go back to work," Tiny told the matron. "I'll take care of these punks."

Danny looked daggers at Izzy.

"You finished?" said Tiny.

Izzy nodded, but he clearly wasn't. His stomach started hurting, and he doubled over and moaned as he laughed.

Joel pleaded, "Will you stop already?"

"I know how to get him to stop," said Tiny. He picked up the phone and dialed. He waited for an answer. Then he said, "Officer Mike? I got a problem here. I may need you to arrest three juvenile delinquents."

It worked. Izzy stopped laughing.

"Okay, thanks, Mike," said Tiny and hung up. "You satisfied?" he asked the boys.

"Are you really gonna have us arrested?" asked Danny.

"Maybe," said Tiny in a voice empty of emotion. "Officer Mike is on his way here to discuss it."

"Please don't arrest us, Tiny," Danny pleaded. "My mother'll kill me."

Danny's calling the manager "Tiny" set Izzy off again, and unable to restrain himself, he held his stomach in painful hysterics.

Joel punched Izzy in the arm. "Enough already!"

The door opened. A policeman entered. He was short and

skinny, with curly red hair.

"Come on in, Mike," said Tiny.

"Are these the criminals?"

"Not only are they causing a disturbance in the theater, but they're laughing at me."

"Not all of us," said Danny in tears. "Just Izzy."

"I'm trying to stop," said Izzy.

"You want me to take them in?" asked Mike.

Tiny was silent. He looked at each one. They all looked terrified.

"You think I should give them another chance?" Tiny asked the officer.

"It's up to you," said Mike. "There's plenty of room in jail."

Tiny looked at the boys with angry eyes and said, "I'm gonna give you another chance, but you're outta my theater. And I don't want you back for a month."

"Okay," said Danny.

"Thanks, Tiny," said Joel.

The mention again of the name sent Izzy again into gales of laughter.

Tiny was furious. "Get the hell out, all of you!"

Officer Mike said, "Come on, punks."

He opened the door, and gestured for them to leave. Danny was out first. Then Joel. Izzy was last, and just before he left, he turned back to Tiny and said, "Are you gonna give us our money back?"

It was Tiny's turn to laugh. "You gotta be kidding."

"We only saw about ten minutes of the picture."

"Get out before I change my mind and have you arrested."

"Come on, Izzy." Joel took his friend by the arm and pulled him out.

Once on the street, the policeman told them to "get goin'

and stay away. If I see you around here again, it's the clink for all of you."

"Come on, guys," said Danny.

"I want my money back," Izzy insisted.

"Will you come on?" Danny repeated, grabbing Izzy by his sleeve.

"I'm not going anywhere until I get my money back. I know my rights."

"Shut up, will you?" said Danny and pulled Izzy away.

As they started towards home, Izzy was furious. "You guys are real sissies," he said. "Why should we lose our money just because we laughed at the movie?"

"*We* didn't laugh," said Danny. "*You and Joel* did."

"I don't know about you guys, but I'm getting my money," Izzy said.

"How?" asked Joel.

"You'll see," said Izzy. And he started off.

"Good luck," said Danny. "I'm going home." He walked away.

Joel was torn. He thought Danny made more sense than Izzy, but Izzy was his best friend. "Wait up, Izzy!" he shouted.

Izzy stopped. Joel caught up to him.

"Where are we going?"

You'll see," said Izzy, and they walked very fast to Izzy's building and up the stairs to his apartment.

"Ma?" he called as he and Joel entered.

Mrs. Peckman appeared from the kitchen wearing an apron over her house dress. "What are you doing home? I thought you went to the movies."

"They kicked us out," said Izzy, "and they wouldn't give us our money back."

"What?" Mrs. Peckman was shocked. "Who kicked you out?"

"The manager," said Joel.

"Why? What did you do?"

"He said we were making noise."

Mrs. Peckman said, "Why didn't he give you your money back?"

"He just wouldn't," said Izzy.

"Take me to him. I'll deal with this." She threw on her coat and said, "Come on."

"You're still wearing your apron, Ma," said Izzy.

"So?" replied Mrs. Peckman. "It's under my coat, isn't it? My *tuchas* isn't showing, is it?" And off she went, led by the boys.

When they reached the theater, Mrs. Peckman walked directly up to the box office and said to the young cashier, "Give them their money back."

The force of Mrs. Peckman's bark took the cashier aback. "I beg your pardon?" she said.

"No, *I* beg *your* pardon," said Mrs. Peckman. "These good boys were thrown out of this theater, but you wouldn't give them their money back."

"There were three of us, Ma. Danny was with us."

"Shush!" said Mrs. Peckman. "Two's enough."

The cashier picked up the phone, dialed, and spoke so that none of them could hear. When she hung up, she told Mrs. Peckman, "The manager will be right out."

"Good!" said Mrs. Peckman.

But before the manager showed up, Officer Mike was there.

"You again?" he said to Joel and Izzy. "Didn't I warn you to stay away from here?"

Mrs. Peckman was surprised. "You know them?"

Joel said, "The manager called him."

Izzy added, "Just because we were laughing."

Mrs. Peckman pointed her finger at the officer and said,

"How dare you take their money for laughing."

Officer Mike, intimidated, explained to Mrs. Peckman that he had nothing to do with that issue. "That's between them and Tiny."

Just then, Tiny appeared.

"Are you Tiny?" Mrs. Peckman asked.

"Who're you?" asked Tiny.

"I'm this one's mother," she said, pointing to Izzy, "and this one's my son's best friend."

"They were misbehavin'. I don't give money back to kids who misbehave."

"Well, I don't pay for my son to go to the movies and not see the movie. Now you give them their money back this minute."

"What if I won't?" asked Tiny. Like Mike, he was intimidated by Mrs. Peckman. Not because she raised her voice—in fact, she spoke quietly—but because you couldn't miss the strength of her determination. And that scared the men.

"What if I won't?" Tiny repeated.

"You *will*," said Mrs. Peckman.

Tiny folded. "Okay," he replied, "but this time only. Next time maybe I'll have them arrested." He looked for confirmation from Officer Mike, but Mike was gone.

Tiny called into the box office, "Give these tough guys their money back, Shirley."

"Here you go," she said to Mrs. Peckman and handed her seventy cents.

Mrs. Peckman counted it, and gave thirty-five cents to Joel, who thanked her profusely, and put the other thirty-five cents under her coat and into her apron pocket. Then she told the boys, "Let's go."

When they were about a block from the movie theater, Mrs. Peckman stopped, turned to Izzy and said, "Come over here." Izzy obeyed. Mrs. Peckman slapped him across the face. Then she turned to Joel. "Now you come here." Joel went to her tentatively. Mrs. Peckman *potched* his behind. "That's for causing trouble," she said and continued homeward. The boys followed. And that was that.

Joel was sixteen and Izzy seventeen when a few of their friends decided one Saturday to go to Fordham Roller Skating Rink and pick up some girls.

One friend, Abie Schneider, said to Izzy, "See you later, pimple-nose," referring to a large pink and purple pimple that had formed on the tip of Izzy's prominent nose.

They agreed to run home, shower, change clothes, and meet at the bus stop in an hour. Izzy was less enthusiastic than the others, and Joel noticed it, but he raced home without discussing it with Izzy.

Lou Sachs was working, Rose was shopping, and Joel's sister Fanny had gone to the movies. Against her will but at her mother's insistence, she had taken their younger sister, Gloria, with her. Joel was alone in the apartment, just out of the shower, and starting to dress when the doorbell rang.

"Okay, just a minute!" he called, and almost broke his neck getting into his underwear and pants. Barefoot and shirtless, not yet fully dry, he hurried to the door and opened it. There was Izzy, who looked as if he'd been crying.

"I'm not going," Izzy said as he entered.

"How come?"

Izzy pointed to the tip of his nose. "You heard what Abie called me."

"Oh, Abie's an ass," said Joel. "What's he talking about? I don't see anything."

"Come off it, you know exactly what he's talking about."

"You mean that little pimple?" said Joel.

"How can I ask a girl to skate? She'll take one look me and laugh in my face."

"Don't be nuts. I didn't even notice it until you pointed it out."

"My mother said it's the worst pimple she ever saw, and I should stop eating so much sweets."

"Nobody will care, Izzy. A lotta kids have pimples."

"*You* don't."

"Sometimes I get blackheads."

"Look, Joel, I'm not going. So forget about it."

"You have to go," Joel insisted. "It's no fun without you."

"I'm not going."

"Aw, Izzy..."

"I hope you have a good time," said Izzy and left.

Joel was upset. It really wouldn't be as much fun without Izzy—he wasn't just saying that. There was something about Izzy that made everyone more alive and everything more fun. As Joel finished getting ready, he thought about Izzy and the sadness his acne caused him. When he looked at Izzy, he didn't see pimples. He saw his best friend. He knew Izzy could be difficult, even a pain in the ass, but none of that had anything to do with his pimples. With a heavy heart, Joel met his other friends at the bus stop, and rode with them to the skating rink.

Just as he was about to buy his ticket, however, he stopped. "I'm not going," he told his friends.

"Whaddya talkin' about?" asked Abie.

"I don't feel so good," Joel said. "I have a stomach ache. I feel like throwing up."

He turned and walked back to the bus stop, while his friends disappeared into the rink. He waited twenty minutes for a bus and then rode back to his neighborhood. He hurried to Izzy's building, climbed the stairs, and rang the bell.

Izzy opened the door. He was picking at a pimple on his forehead. Surprised to see Joel, he asked, "What are you doing here?"

"I changed my mind about going."

"How come?"

"I told you: it's no fun for me without you around. Let's go to the movies instead."

"Who's there, Izzy?" called Mrs. Peckman from the kitchen.

"It's me, Mrs. Peckman," Joel called.

"We're going to the movies," called Izzy.

"Don't get into trouble."

"For cryin' out loud, Ma, that only happened once, a long time ago!"

"Just don't let it happen again."

Izzy scowled and said to Joel, "Let's get out of here."

Those were Joel's strongest memories of Izzy as he prepared to meet him for lunch after fifty years. He cherished those memories. He knew he would find a different Izzy today, and he wondered if this one would still be special? Would he be as compassionate? As liberal? As funny looking? And what would Izzy think of *him*?

He grew more and more excited as he approached the restaurant. When he was about half a block away, he spotted an old man walking with a cane a short distance ahead of him. He knew, without even seeing his face, that the white-haired man, stooped over almost in half, limping very slowly, and carefully dragging his right foot, was Izzy. Joel slowed his pace. He followed Izzy through the door of the restaurant, and watched with profound sadness as his old friend negotiated the stairs. The climb was extremely difficult for him, although he persisted, as if he was determined to defeat the stairs before they got the better of him.

As he watched Izzy ascend the stairs, breathless, moving more and more slowly, he remembered something Mrs. Kalenson, his sixth-grade teacher had told the class: "A best friend is someone you cherish for life." But Joel realized he couldn't face a reunion with Izzy. He could handle change, but not ruin.

He turned around and went back home.

Acknowledgments

Although I've been a writer my entire career, most of my writing has consisted of plays, teleplays, and screenplays. Over the years, I've written a few short stories. But *Out of the Bronx* is my first prose collection, and to see it through, I felt insecure enough to need a good deal of encouragement. And I received it.

From my wife, Delia Ephron, who is a seasoned writer of many great collections, novels, screenplays, essays, and plays. She is also a tough and brilliant critic. Not only did she read my stories more than once and criticize them (more than once) but she also encouraged me every step of the way along this unfamiliar journey of writing a book. Nothing was more important or comforting to me than her encouragement. She provided plenty of that.

My dear friend, Bob Wallace, who is the best editor I could have hoped for. He had the courage to start a publishing company at a time when publishing is a highly risky business. It was he who responded to my work as if he were Jewish (and, in fact, corrected the spelling of many Yiddish words I had misspelled), convinced me to write my book of stories, and offered to publish it. He has since edited each draft with extraordinary attention and devotion.

Bob Asahina, who is Bob Wallace's friend and business partner—and now my friend and co-editor. I don't know Asahina as well as I know Wallace, but he appreciated my work enough to agree to its publication, so how can I feel anything but fondness for him and gratitude to him?

Margot Frankel, who designed the perfect cover, and who, despite my making endless demands on her time and talent, never lost patience with me.

Ruth Graham, who not only corrected the mechanics of my work, but also improved the quality of my writing in so many ways.

Eva Guralnick, whose elegant interior design of the book seems to me to add distinction to the work.

Many friends whom I asked to read one or more stories herein. They include Susannah Grant, Philip Johnston, Lawrence Levine, and Alessandro Tannaka, four of my former and most talented screenwriting students; Jessie Nelson, a wonderful writer/director, who shone in one of my early plays as an actress when both of us were very young; Courtney Gatewood, the wife of another of my former students and the mother of my godson, a woman of intelligence, appreciation and sensitivity about writing; Deena Goldstone, one of my oldest and dearest friends, who coincidentally is having her first book, also a collection of short stories, published in the spring of 2014; Patricia Crown, my brilliant and generous attorney; Adam and Julie Kass, my treasured children; Gail Kass and Roy Friedman, my devoted sister and brother-in-law; Patricia Williams, my favorite portrait photographer, who alone takes good pictures of me; Holly Palance; Heather Chaplin; Marie Brenner; Lisa Weinstein; Diane Sokolow; Cherie Nowlan; Julia Gregson; Richard Gregson; Jenny Snider; Joel Mason, and Seth Swoboda.

Thank you all.

ABOUT THE AUTHOR

Jerome Kass is an Emmy nominee and Writers Guild Award winner for his CBS special, *Queen of the Stardust Ballroom*, which starred Maureen Stapleton and Charles Durning. Kass later adapted it to the Broadway stage. Michael Bennett (*A Chorus Line*) produced and directed it as *Ballroom*. Kass was nominated for a Tony for that production. The stage production is now being prepared for a revival in England in the fall of 2014.

Other television specials and movies of the week written by Kass include *A Brand New Life*, for which Cloris Leachman won an Emmy; *My Old Man*, which starred Warren Oates and Eileen Brennan; *The Fighter*, starring Gregory Harrison; *Scorned and Swindled*, with Tuesday Weld and Keith Carradine; the mini-series *Evergreen*, starring Lesley Ann Warren, Armand Assante, and Ian McShane; *Crossing To Freedom* (aka *Pied Piper*), with Peter O'Toole and Mare Winningham; *Last Wish*, with Patty Duke and Maureen Stapleton; *The Only Way Out*, with Henry Winkler and John Ritter; and *Secrets*, with Veronica Hamel, Richard Kiley and Julie Harris.

Kass co-wrote the feature film *The Black Stallion Returns*, produced by Francis Ford Coppola for United Artists.

His theater work includes *Monopoly*, an evening of four one-act plays, which featured Estelle Parsons; the play, *Saturday Night*; the musical *Norman's Ark*, and *Ballroom*, starring Dorothy Loudon and Vincent Gardenia.

Kass adapted three classic musicals to concert versions for *Reprise!* (the *Encores* of the West) in Los Angeles: *Finian's Rainbow* with Andrea Marcovicci, *Pajama Game* with Christine Ebersol, and *Fiorello* with Tony Danza.

He has taught screenwriting at the American Film Institute, the Tisch School of the Arts at NYU, and at the Film School of Columbia University.

Kass was born in Chicago, grew up in the Bronx, is married to Delia Ephron, and has two children, Julie and Adam.

CPSIA information can be obtained at www.ICGtesting.com
Printed in the USA
BVOW03s0239040314

346600BV00001B/2/P